HENCEFORTH

Clouds hold the water drawn from the ocean,
but it is the clouds to which people look.
                                    - Jnaneshwar

PROJECT EDITOR
Mini Krishnan

GENERAL EDITOR
C. D. Narasimhaiah

CHIEF EDITORS

Bengali	:	**Nabaneeta Dev Sen**
Gujarati	:	**Suresh Dalal**
Hindi	:	**Jai Ratan**
Kannada	:	**Ramachandra Sharma**
Malayalam	:	**K. M. George**
Marathi	:	**Makarand Paranjape**
Oriya	:	**Manoj Das**
Punjabi	:	**Darshan Singh Maini**
Tamil	:	**C. T. Indra**
Telugu	:	**A. V. Krishna Rao**
Urdu	:	**Balraj Komal**

Harindra Dave
HENCEFORTH
(Anagat)

Translated from the Gujarati original by
BHARATI DAVE

First Published 1996

MACMILLAN INDIA LIMITED

Madras Jaipur Patna Bombay Bangalore Bhopal
Coimbatore Cuttack Guwahati Hubli Hyderabad
Lucknow Madurai Nagpur Trivandrum Visakhapatnam
Associated companies throughout the world

SBN 033392 312 X

Typeset at Laserwords, Madras 600 020
Cover Picture coordination: The Gallery, Madras 600 006

Published by
Rajiv Beri for Macmillan India Limited, 21 Patullos Road
Madras 600 002 and Printed by V.N. Rao at
Macmillan India Press, Madras-600 041

About this series

Whatever our quarrels and shifting factions, all Indians know that they have a complex, stable system of values, beliefs and practices which — though forged long ago — has never really been interrupted. It still underlines the surface differences and makes them comprehensible. Our programme of translations is an exploration of this Indian tradition which is one of humankind's most enduring attempts to create an order of existence that would make life both tolerable and meaningful.

The method we have adopted is to translate selections from the corpus of fiction Indians have created after their Independence (1947). It is our hope that these novels will express most of the ideas, customs, unquestioned assumptions and the persistent doubts that have characterised Indian life for at least a thousand years, and, more recently, after the impact of western ways of thinking on it.

Novels from Telugu, Tamil, Kannada, Malayalam, Gujarati, Oriya, Marathi, Punjabi, Urdu, Bengali and Hindi have been selected. We hope to include more Indian languages in the next phase.

This project has been made possible by the generosity of MR. AR. Educational Trust, of which Sri A.M.M. Arunachalam is the Trustee. Known to us, there has never been such a big and systematic programme of translations sponsored by the private sector.

Some of the footnotes may seem excessive, but they have been prepared with non-Indian readers in mind.

MINI KRISHNAN
Project Editor

INTRODUCTION

The word "anagat" (hereafter) leads to two supplementary words: "aagat" and "vigat". The time past is "vigat"; the time present, which flows swiftly, is "aagat"; and the time future is "anagat". Thus time has been divided into three parts. But can time really be divided? T.S. Eliot in his poem *Four Quartets* said:

Time past and time future
What might have been and what has been
Point to one end, which is always present.

These three distinct time-frames do not appear sequentially. Any one time-frame includes the other two. They are interwoven.

It may be asked, what has this analysis of time to do with a novel? A novel mostly consists of characters and events. It is a story of happy or unhappy events in the lives of various individuals. Where then, is the need to bring in this complex philosophical riddle of time?

The reason is, today the novel has already crossed its traditional bounds and encroached upon the fields of philosophy and poetry. The novel does not merely reflect life or provide a sketch of characters or narrate events; but, using traditional devices, poses questions as to what life is and why it is so. It also tries to find the answers. Exploration into an unknown area with the help of the old tools of fiction is a new literary experiment. In the modern literary environment, there are few novelists who have taken up the challenge. In my view, the author of this significant novel has not only assumed this challenge but has met it successfully.

The author takes us into this world's absurd time-frame and incompatible characters. Tired of the strenuous life of the city, the protagonist sets off alone to the village, Urad, situated on the seashore. He wants only a few hours of relaxation. He wants to ponder over his relationship with Manjari with whom he is in love. He enters this village near Daman where life is free from tension. The only thing he experiences here is the immensity of the sea; he feels time has almost stopped.

In this world of arrested time, the protagonist encounters different people with "arrested lives". Here he meets an old man who had, decades ago, lost his wife in an earthquake: he had then, in utter despair, tried to end his own life by drowning himself. But he returned after walking a long distance in knee-deep water. Now all alone, more like a foreigner than a native in his own place, he seemed cut off from his surroundings. The agony of this old man sets the background for this novel. Later in the novel, when Tikekar's daughter-in-law sings a mediaeval lyric, "I have already seen my death with my own eyes: I am in the twilight of life, just a foreigner", one not only remembers this old man but also feels that each individual of the village feels the notes of this sad lyric reverberating within him. Chhanalal who once attained popularity on the city-stage, now managing a travelling troupe; the young and pretty daughter of Jeevalal who has lost sense of her youth and life; Tikekar and his daughter-in-law (who live outside the area of normal social relationships) a Parsee doctor who, not being able to save his own son, tries to help all the patients of the village; it can also be Christine, deserted by her husband, who could not stand the sight of a white patch on her breasts. Still, all these characters continue to live. Why? For what sort of future? Is there any meaning in continuing to live in such anguish?

One meaning is provided by Father Vallant to whom Christine goes for confession. Jesus had to carry his own cross and when he was not able to move because of its unbearable weight Roman soldiers had lashed him. At that time, Jesus's distressed eyes, which blended the flame of life along with the darkness of certain death, are for us perhaps a signal of the way we should look at life.

Another meaning can be read through the life of the stage artist, Chhanalal, who, while off-stage, looks ragged and broken, but, when pushed on to a stage, transforms into a king who, through his sonorous voice resounding with princely pride, evokes spontaneous applause. Do we also live two lives, one offstage and another on stage? Which is our real life?

Two more strange images emerge from this novel. A man standing on an iceberg in the sea believes that he has saved himself from drowning. But the iceberg — his very support — is gradually melting into the sea. The other image is from *Jnaneshwari* (Saint Jnaneshwar's exposition of the *Gita* in Marathi): "One does not known when the lamp in a covered waterpot extinguishes: just like that you must leave the body with no one noticing how the light went off."

At the beginning of the novel, the protagonist's life is just like a flame hidden in a covered earthen pot. He has been bitten by a snake. The snake-charmer feels that he has only forty-eight hours to live. Dr. Meherwan feels he can save him. If he dies — well, everything dies, but by chance if he lives — what will happen to Manjari, his beloved whom he left behind in the city? What will happen to Christine? Those basic questions of life are more painful than the snake-bite. The novel ends with this question. Rather, it can be said that the author ends the novel by depicting time as a question mark. This end is a starting point of a new series of questions.

Ultimately, amidst all these, is there any one factor that emerges intact? Perturbed by this question, I try to take refuge in poetry and come across a few lines of Ezra Pound:

What thou lovest well, remains, the rest is dross,
What thou lovest well shall not bereft from thee
What thou lovest well is thy true heritage.

Perhaps, the poet is telling the truth; but is not love also a flame hidden under a covered vessel that may go out unnoticed?

This is a piercing question. There it is. You may wonder why an Introduction should end with a question rather than a reconciliation? But what can be done? The introduction to a novel that ends in a question also has to take refuge in that eternal question: Is there any other alternative?

DHARMVEER BHARATI

Only twenty-four hours left now, he thought and laughed. The sea was roaring, but the sound was drowned by the noise of the wind passing through the cypress trees. His laughter had silenced the other two sounds, startling him.

Only twenty-four hours left?

He remembered the snake-charmer. He remembered all the tricks he had performed, and the incense smoke he had created! How suffocating it had been! Just remembering it brought a choking sensation! He coughed and took a deep breath; and the salty humid air that came from the sea stuck in his throat!

The snake-charmer was awesome. He had twined a green cloth around himself and worn a saffron cloak over it. He had justified his mode of dress by calling himself a saint and a fakir. He carried a snake-charmer's flute in one hand and a basket in the other which contained an image of his family deity.[1]

He had taken something from the pocket of his loose cloak and thrown it into the burning firepan. Instantly the whole atmosphere had filled with smoke, clouding all vision. His incoherent utterances penetrated the smoke; again he flung something into the glowing pan and a flame leapt upward.

"Be patient, be patient, my God, be patient," he had muttered, repeatedly and incoherently.

The smoke had looked strange. It soothed his pain while increasing his sense of suffocation. Or was it that the increasing suffocation caused him to forget his pain?

When the smoke subsided a little, he could see the snake-charmer taking the snake out from its basket. He placed its swaying hood on his palm and talked to the reptile. The snake nodded as if it had understood the language of the snake-charmer.

"Very good, my God, very good!" said the snake-charmer whose head was also swaying. "Yes, you had better ask your

_____

[1] the guardian diety of the family.

thousand hooded grandfather who stays beyond the region of the seven seas." Then he whispered against the snake's hood and threw something in the firepan again filling the whole hut with smoke.

This time, the smell of the smoke was milder but sweet. As the flames died down, he took a piece of burning coal in his hand as if he were playing with a flower, brought it near his lips, mumbled something over it and put it on the poisonous sting on Aalok's leg.

Though Aalok did not feel the pain of it, he had screamed in fear, as he was aware of the burning coal being placed on his leg.

The snake-charmer laughed heartily. He gave the snake a flying kiss. "God, be seated," he said. The cobra, as if understanding his language, contracted its hood, curled its body and withdrew. The snake-charmer closed the basket.

The echoes of loud laughter had not faded from his heart. He looked curiously at the snake-charmer who said: "It is the gift from the water deity[1] — part of which has gone into the fire, but part of it still remains inside you. I have understood its speed. It will pass through the veins; through all the fifty-six crores of veins; it will race and reach the umbilicus after forty-eight hours, and at that time, I cannot say what will happen."

"What do you mean?"

"It will be as the Almighty wishes ……. At present, it is moving through the ten thousandth vein[2]. Once its circle is over in the umbilicus and if the umbilical plexus is not able to digest the gift from the deity, then wait for your doom, but if it is digested then …."

"Then what?"

"Then this fakir will kiss your feet. Though I have heard about such lucky people, I have hardly come across a single such person!"

"That means the poison will not pass out?"

"Don't say poison, Babu, it is not poison, it is the gift from the deity. This deity, the king of water, stays at the bottom of

2

---

[1] refers to Varun the water deity according to India's Vedic tradition.
[2] according to Yoga Shastra a body has as many as seventy-two thousand veins.

the sea in a white cave made up of sea shells, and hardly ever emerges to give his blessings! With those blessings, even if life ends, death will be a worthy reward ......"

"Death ......" his lips trembled a little.

"Babu, is life so very dear? You have been gifted a life of forty-eight hours ...... what will happen to me? My life can end even the next moment! Only a lucky person has such a long life!"

He could smile now, remembering the whole episode. Forty-eight hours of life, of which twenty-four had already passed!

He had almost forgotten why he had come here, to the beach at Urad. He had come here just to wander about. He had decided to get married ... and at the last moment the wedding had been postponed. Some uncle of Manjari's had expired, and the wedding could not take place. Aalok was completely at a loss and had felt a vacuum forming within. On the night they were to be married, he had gone through the moments they had been together. Now it all looked so very ridiculous!

It was true that during weak moments he craved feminine company, but by and large, he had never felt the real need for a woman in his life. The time he had spent with Manjari and the incessant talk they had had were so futile! The words "I love you" were like a gas balloon which bursts in mid-air! He still remembered chronologically, everything that had happened when he had taken Manjari's soft hand in his and said so many things!

On the evening of the day they were to be married, he had met Manjari.

"How different the day could have been ...!" Manjari had said.

"Yes ......" he had replied.

"Why are you so quiet?" Manjari had asked.

"Oh, just nothing! I am listening."

"But what are you listening to? I am not talking," Manjari had said.

"I am listening to all the words that we spoke in the past!"

"Do you remember them?"

"Who knows? It seems I've forgotten even those words which I once remembered."

"Why so?" Manjari had looked at him with concern, and Aalok had laughed. He had said: "Come, let us go for a movie."

"Oh, no, it has been only eight days since uncle's death. If somebody sees us in the theatre ......"

"Manjari!"

Manjari had looked up.

"You have so many relatives — people who might be called yours; your uncle, father, mother, brother, sister, aunty, cousins ...... don't you sometimes get lost amongst them?"

"Oh no, on the contrary I would feel lonely without them."

"You come from such a large family, and I have nobody in my house ...... won't you feel suffocated?"

"But you will be there!"

"Will I? Who knows?"

Aalok had sighed and Manjari had left with a heavy heart.

On that very night, he had taken a local train to Urad Road. A fellow resident at the hostel had mentioned that the sea there was unique. He used to say that there were only three beaches worth seeing in the whole world! One was in Brighton, the second was the Marina in Madras, and the third was the beach at Urad in Gujarat ....

The train reached Urad Road and he got down.

The train left the station. The lights of the platform were getting dim when he went to the exit and asked, "I want to go to the village. When can I get a bus?"

"The bus service starts at eight in the morning — after the arrival of the seven-thirty train," said the station master.

"Any waiting room here?" Aalok asked, though he had not seen one.

"No, but there are benches occupied by those rogues from the village — come on, get up," the station master poked a youth awake with the stick he carried. The boy got up rubbing his eyes.

"Let him sleep," said Aalok.

"You don't know these thieves. Come on, get up, let this sahib sleep," said the station master. Aalok was perplexed. The boy got up and rolled his bedding, his eyes still full of sleep. He unrolled his bedding near the wall glancing fearfully at the station master and then at Aalok.

"You may sleep sir," said the station master.

"But that boy ......"

"He will lie down there. Don't pity him. Animal—he is an animal ....." The station master got busy with the work of the on-coming goods train and began instructing his men.

Aalok continued to stand there. He felt as if there was still the ghost of somebody's sleep, lying on the bench. He looked around; all the benches were occupied. The boy was sitting on his blanket, looking at him. Aalok looked at him and asked, "Do you want to sleep here?" The boy shook his head vehemently.

Aalok went near the bench. He took out a handkerchief from his pocket, cleaned the bench and made a pillow of his bag before he lay down.

"Where will you stay in Urad, sir?" The station master inquired after returning with an orderly.

"I am not sure."

"No?"

"All that I want to do here is to find peace, write something. Somebody suggested that the beach of Urad is very good and that I should go and stay there ......".

"Yes, but did he not tell you everything?"

"Regarding what?"

"Where to stay, where not to. He told you nothing?"

Aalok shook his head, and all of a sudden he remembered the boy who was asked to vacate the bench. He had been about to go to sleep again but listening to the station master's voice, he had got up again and shivered, covering himself with the sheet.

"There are only three beaches in the world—Brighton, Marina and Urad ......"

Aalok remembered his hostel friend.

The station master was watching carefully the effect of his own words. He added, "otherwise it is a dying village—full of old people, widows, orphaned children ......"

"Oh, is that so?" Aalok queried for the sake of saying something.

This encouragement was enough for the station master. He became eloquent: "Sir, there is no business here now. Once upon a time there were such unique fishes in the sea, you couldn't find them anywhere else. Once I saw with my own eyes a fish twenty-five feet long. Gafur had caught it." His look measured Aalok from head to toe; he added, "say about, four times your length."

Aalok felt he should say something. But his eyes went to the boy who had slept curled up and whose eyes had just opened. His mind on the boy, Aalok forgot to reply.

The station master waited for a reply for some time and not receiving any, continued undaunted. "This is a heaven for fisherfolk and sir," he almost whispered, "You like to drink, don't you?"

"No," Aalok said with a start.

"Then your trip has no meaning!"

"Why?"

"Since the Daman port[1] became operative, our business has dropped, but the natives used to brew such nice toddy that though there was strict prohibition, the policemen used to come here — not to arrest anybody, but to collect instalments of the bribe. The policemen on this beat were getting more money than their pay through these instalments — those days are gone now. Now they get it in the open market in Daman, so why should they come here secretly?"

"Right," he replied curtly.

"You do like this village — but you do not drink, otherwise you would have enjoyed staying in the hut of Jeeva Kalal. Do not even go near those boarding houses of Kathiawadi and Christian people. One is in Viramgaum and very cunning while the other will not peel his glance off your pocket — You haven't got plenty with you to be at any risk, have you?"

The boy slightly removed the linen from his face, as if to listen to the answer to that question. There was movement on the other

---

[1] a free port, formerly a Portuguese colony in the West Coast of India, now a part of Gujarat.

benches too. Aalok felt uneasy and was drenched in perspiration. He did have a little wealth but no capital. He knew that in such unknown places, money was his only support.

"Oh no, sir," said he, laughing foolishly. "I hardly have fifteen-twenty rupees for the return ticket!"

After this talk, the station master lost interest in this passenger. He felt that the movements on the other benches too had stopped. He closed his eyes. Somewhere a bird was chirping. Somewhere somebody coughed harshly; the wind made funny noises in the branches and he felt as if somebody was laughing. He opened his eyes and sat up. Suddenly the station was quiet. He lay down once again, only to be woken up startled, feeling somebody's deep breathing in his ear. With an effort he suppressed a scream that arose within him. He put his hand on his pocket. The deep breathing was still in his ear. He had no courage to open his eyes but he heard the distant sound of an in-coming train and the movements in the station gave him some peace and assurance. He opened his eyes. A white dog was standing near him, breathing heavily his tongue hanging out. The animal looked surprised at seeing a stranger on the bench. The goods train whistled passed the station and he heaved a sigh of relief. Aalok drove the dog away and once again tried to get back to sleep.

T WO

The scenario changed in the morning. Two shepherd women were squatting on the platform, with pieces of cloth covering their milk vessels. A number of people sat on the benches — a farmer, a businessman, and a vagabond. He got up bewildered. He looked around in confusion. Had he got up from the same bench where he had slept the previous night? Almost everyone was staring at him as if he were an animal that had wandered out of a circus. He made sure that his clothes were in order. Then he remembered the boy and at the same time his pocket. While checking his pocket, he simultaneously looked at the opposite wall. His gaze met that of the young shepherd women sitting across. That boy was no longer there but the money in his pocket was safe.

"Sir, may I polish your shoes?" said a boy approaching him gingerly.

He tried to identify whether this boy was the same as the one he had displaced the night before. His silence was taken as assent and the boy started brushing his shoes.

"Have you been to school?" He asked a routine question usually asked by city people.

"Oh yes!" The boy was used to such routine questions, it seemed.

"Upto what class?"

"Enough to read and write letters."

"When will the bus service start from here?"

"Where to, sir?"

"Urad ......"

"I saw the bus at the stand. It will start after the morning train arrives. But you had better take your seat before the train gets in, or else, once the passengers begin to arrive, you will hardly get a seat; and the bus gets terribly overcrowded."

Aalok put on his gleaming shoes, walked round the platform once and came out. Someone who looked like a businessman tried to draw his attention as if he wanted to ask him something like "Where do you want to go?" "Urad? ...." Eventually he won Aalok's attention.

"Yes, Urad."

"Where will you stay?"

"Boarding House."

"Gujarati or Christian?"

"Which one is better?"

"Better go to Patel's Boarding House. At least you will get good food. If you want to enjoy ......" putting a finger on his lips he said, "Christians are better ...... but our Patel also keeps it, though he is not a connoisseur of the stuff. He gives country stuff in Diplomat bottles."

"What stuff do you prefer?" Aalok asked.

At which his dislike was plain and he looked at Aalok in disgust as if he had asked a very personal question. Then he said, "Come, the bus has already arrived."

"Are you going to Urad?"

"No, I am going on business."

"What is your business?"

"Business? What business has remained here now? The city people have taken away a great deal! And whatever has remained, the government has taken away. What are we to do? Where are we to go leaving our place of origin?"

"Which is your native place?"

"This very place!" and he slipped away saying, "Let me check whether the tickets have begun to be issued."

Aalok was enjoying himself. This person who had wanted to know every detail about him, had not answered a single question about himself! Aalok was tempted to ask more questions — but then, that was probably the reason for his moving away abruptly.

Aalok was about to board the bus when the conductor almost stopped him saying, "Let the train arrive ......" but then he became aware of the way Aalok was dressed and, said instead "It is all right, sir, you may sit."

But he did not admit the two milkmaids with their vessels, saying, "Can't you see there is still time?"

As he climbed into the bus, Aalok suddenly remembered the boy on the bench who looked like a ghost and he felt a heaviness that equalled the heaviness with which he had slept on the bench. In the bus he chose a window seat.

The station was now bustling with activity. He tried to locate the tree whose branches had made those funny noises last night. He was not able to locate the ghost or the tree but the white dog was still panting, its tongue hanging out. Aalok remembered how he had been frightened the night before and laughed at himself.

Once the train arrived, the passengers rushed for places on the bus. Aalok realised that the conductor had really obliged him by allowing him to take his seat in the bus before the arrival of the train. He observed that the conductor was unperturbed by the rush outside. Before selling a ticket, he would first scrutinise the passenger's face and then take the fare. There followed the routine question about destination before he handed over the ticket.

Aalok's fellow passenger's breath stank. Aalok's satisfaction with his window seat vanished even before others could enter the bus. He felt like giving up his seat to an old woman, but looking at her wrinkled and angry face, he decided otherwise. He saw that she had already quarrelled with the conductor about some small change.

At last the bus began to move.

The road was bad and the bus bumped along laboriously. Aalok who was sick felt even more ill because of the acrid and sour stench all around him. He was relieved when the fellow passenger next to him got down at the next stop. And in his place sat the old woman who was still grumbling and abusing the conductor.

"Sir, may I have your luggage?" somebody said and took the bag from his hand. "Is there any other baggage?"

"No, this is all," said Aalok.

"Where do you want to go?"

"Christian Boarding house ..." Aalok uttered the first name that came to his lips.

He was received by a barking dog, followed by a gentle voice calling "Tommy-Tommy." A woman came out adjusting her apron. She must have been very beautiful in her youth. She looked dignified and her features were well chiselled. For a second she stared at Aalok and then smiled.

"Welcome," she said.

Opening a room, she instructed the man who held the baggage, "Keep the luggage here."

Then she addressed Aalok: "Please make yourself comfortable. I'll send in tea and snacks. Would you like to have a hot bath now or after some time?" Aalok gave the necessary instructions.

Before leaving she opened the back door and the side window. "There is a nice verandah where you might place the armchair."

Aalok turned round and observed the room when she left. A mirror stood on a writing table so that it could double as a dressing table. There was a cot strung with a mosquito net, two chairs, and the armchair in the verandah. It was made of black ebony, and it reminded him of a sketch by a well-known artist, Ravishankar Rawal, who had depicted a similar type of an armchair in a drawing room. A few steps away from the verandah was the sea. Some cypress trees made the view enchanting. To the left of the room, there was a door which opened into the bathroom.

He sat on the cot and thought about how strangely he had behaved with Manjari. Perhaps she would ring him and learn that he had not gone to the office; then she would go to his home and see that it was locked from the outside.

She'd certainly be worried. Her father, mother and aunt too would be worried. She would then make an effort to forget everything. But of course, before that she would try to telephone him and go to his place.

And by that time, he would also get used to the new situation, get engrossed in the daily routine and forget himself.

Before he could start his meal, the manageress of the Boarding House came in and sat on the chair that was before his.

It was then that Aalok observed her calmly. She could be called beautiful even now. She looked between twenty-five and forty, depending on the man who looked at her. He observed the few strands of gray in her buff coloured hair; her almond-shaped eyes were the same colour.

"My name is Christine," she said, smiling faintly, "Christine Wellworth."

"My name is Aalok, just Aalok. The atmosphere here is very pleasant," said Aalok.

"Do you like it?" asked Christine. "Many people get tired of being alone, but I like this quiet atmosphere. I have stayed here almost alone for the last twelve years."

Aalok did not know what to say, so instead of answering her, he said, "Why don't you eat with me?"

"No, not today. Perhaps if you stay on, we will have our meals together. How is the cooking? Do you like it?"

"It is fine," he said, trying to gulp down the dry and tasteless chappati[1] with great difficulty.

---

[1] unleavened bread, made of wheat flour and cooked in an open fire.

"Is this your first visit to this place?"

"Yes."

"Any particular reason?"

"Yes — only to rest."

Christine stared at Aalok steadily. Though Aalok's eyes were fixed on his plate, he could feel her stare.

"Is there anybody else here at this time?" he asked.

"No, why should anybody come here at this time? Now that Daman is open who would want to come here?"

"Such a beautiful place and no one knows its importance?" asked Aalok.

"Mr. Aalok, dare I mention it? If you but once drink the toddy distilled here, you would forget all superior kinds of rum. It is a real man's drink ..."

"Unfortunately, I will not be able to take advantage of that," said Aalok laughingly. "But I have been hearing its praises sung ever since I reached the platform at the railway station."

"Earlier, we used to get many customers during this time of the year, and we had to pitch tents on the ground to accommodate them. But ever since this Daman Port was opened ..."

"It seems, in the life of this village, Daman is a living character; so many people have mentioned that name since my arrival."

THREE

Perhaps this was Christine's first encounter with this kind of talk from a customer. She looked curiously at Aalok and changed the topic.

In the afternoon, Aalok lay back in the armchair on the verandah, eyes closed. His legs were propped up on the stool opposite. It was high tide and he could hear the rhythmic sound of the waves. Two small children stood on the shore with their fishing bait in the water. Their shouts reached him. The rattle of washing plates came from the well nearby. The sound of water being drawn was also audible. All these sounds merged with one another, and Aalok felt as if he were hearing them for the first time. For some time he sat there, then restless, he got up, went in and sat on the chair by the table. He took up his pen intending to write something. He observed that another Aalok, reflected in the mirror, had also taken pen in hand and was thinking of writing something! Aalok enjoyed looking at that face. There were certain lines on that face which Aalok saw for the first time. His forehead was a little broader. His ruffled hair shone black. His eyes though deep-seated and sad, looked clear and rested. Both cheeks were dimpled and his red lips looked like a flat line, pressed firmly. Aalok looked at himself curiously, with both dread and some confusion.

Staring at himself for such a long time in the mirror made him fearful. He remembered an elderly person who had once said, "You will go mad" to the boy Aalok as he sat staring at his reflection in the mirror. Today, he felt that some part of his self from within was telling him, "Perhaps you will go mad." But inspite of this warning he continued to stare at the reflection with great concentration, as if he had never encountered himself before.

He was awakened from that trance only when the pen slipped from his fingers. He picked up his pen and just then saw a boy with a tea tray in his hands.

"Come in," said Aalok.

The boy looked about fifteen years old. His open mouth was almost like a smile, or was it blankness? He placed the tray on the table and turned to leave.

"Boy!" Aalok called.

He turned back.

"What is your name?"

"Shankar."

"You work here?"

"Yes." He wanted to say something more but stopped.

"Don't you have parents?"

"I do; they stay in the village." There were many questions Aalok wanted to ask, but he did not feel like prolonging the conversation so he allowed Shankar to go away.

When he went down to the seashore, the sand was wet, the receding tide had marked the surface with varied designs made by tiny crabs and small insects. It looked as if some artist had worked his art on the sands. Though he wanted to go near the sea, he turned back as he did not like to crush the insects underfoot.

He sat on the dry sand of the beach. The sand here was fine, good enough to tempt anybody to build a castle. He too would have perhaps started building one, but he heard footsteps. An old man stood behind him. He looked curiously at Aalok and then said, "You are new here. Have you arrived recently?"

"This is my first visit," answered Aalok.

Looking at Aalok's welcoming glance, the old man sat down beside him. After a long time he seemed to have finally met somebody on this lonely beach, who would in all probability, listen to his tale.

"How long will you be staying?"

"I am not sure, but I am here for some time," said Aalok.

"You are staying at the Christian Hotel, aren't you?"

"Yes."

"You had better be cautious about your daily bills, clarify from the start — the lady has a very sweet tongue, but she has been in this business for the past twelve years ..."

"What is your profession?" Aalok asked in order to change the subject.

"What is there to do here? From this seashore to home and from home to the seashore ...... gone are those days now, brother. Can you see that new building in the east? Our houses were there in the old days. The family of Pathak was supposed to be a very cultured one," he said, looking at the three storeyed building that had come up on the eastern side. His eyes were not looking at the building but were scanning past events. Aalok stared at the wrinkled face of the old man, and he remembered the delicate designs made by insects on the wet sand. Years, time and God had etched similar designs on the face of the old man. Aalok was anxious to bring back the old man from his nostalgic thoughts which lay entwined with that building, and so he called out "Dada,[1] Dada!"

---

[1] equivalent for grandfather/a way of addressing an old person respectfully.

"Oh yes?" The old man replied with a melancholy smile.

"Is this sea dangerous?" asked Aalok.

"Dangerous? No, not at all. You can walk straight into it for furlongs and the water will still be just knee-deep. If you want to commit suicide, you would surely change your mind and return ...."

Aalok felt that he should try and walk that distance to get enough time to decide about suicide!

He looked with unwavering concentration at the old man who grew uneasy under his stare. There was a trace of fear in his eyes, he felt somebody was trying to reach deep into him to peel off the layers to find his secret.

"Did you ever try to commit suicide in this sea?" asked Aalok, perceptively.

The fearful eyes fell under closed lids and for a long while, he did not speak.

The sound of the receding tide alone broke the silence and the sea receded farther and farther away. Aalok played with the sand as if expecting no answer. The silence around deepened and the roar of the sea intensified. At a distance, a few boys were trying to fly a kite. The shadows of the evening grew long and the sand cold.

The old man could no longer bear the silence; he said, "Yes, once."

Aalok looked curiously at the old man. He was stunned by the unexpected reply.

The old man took some time to collect himself. He then said in a whisper, "Yes, once I did go in there intending to commit suicide ...."

The atmosphere suddenly turned gloomy. The children were silently drawing in the string from their torn kites. The tide had receded into the vast sea.

"Why?" asked Aalok. The past came rushing into the old man's mind and he relived that particular night: "You may not even have been born at that time," the old man began. "I had quarrelled with my wife Gomti that night and she had made her bed separately in the far corner of the room; she slept alone, curled up, and facing the wall." He tried to recollect events of that night. Angry and obstinate he too had slept facing the opposite wall. He was not aware how and when he slept, but when he awoke, the sea was roaring as if in a storm. He rose confused, as he felt somebody was rocking him to and fro; and some deep seated fury from the heart yearned for self-expression. Gomti, who was sleeping a little away from him was also moving. She was looking at the ceiling with fearful eyes.

After some time, he realised that it was the tremor of an earthquake, and not the sound of the sea. The noise became more and more dreadful: the sound of the frightened birds in the trees and the sound of the sea grew louder and deeper than before. Suddenly a tremendous shattering noise ripped through the air.

"G ... O ... M ... T ... i-i-i," he shouted and Gomti who suddenly tried to get up from her bed was thrown back — the earth which bore her person, suddenly gave way, and along with her bed, she vanished down the chasm created by the collapse of the floor.

The tremors of the earthquake stopped but he was trembling from top to toe. His eyes dripped fear and stared as if he were trying to locate Gomti who was about to get up, but was swallowed whole by the earth! He could still hear that loud cracking of the earth! It was as if that sound still reverberated in his stunned heart! His lips twisted and his throat turned dry. Around him lay the bricks from the demolished walls. Suddenly a heavy load fell on him knocking him unconscious.

"When I woke up, I was in a military camp,[1]" said the old man.

As if he had heard that tremendous cracking sound, Aalok too was trembling all over, his face pale, eyes lifeless.

"The first thing I did after regaining consciousness was to enquire after Gomti. But there was not a single familiar face who could tell me anything about her. Half the town was buried. Some were in makeshift military hospitals and the few who were saved from this catastrophe had migrated to other villages," said the old man.

When he recovered fully, he remembered the day very well. He had strict orders from the doctor to rest, but instead he had attempted to go out.

---

[1] a temporary hospital or shelter raised by the military to assist during natural calamity.

And how many times the young soldier at the door had stopped him! Nobody answered him satisfactorily. The doctor had come once and gone away. The soldiers who were looking after the sick were not talking to him, but the way they talked amongst themselves showed their anguish and pain. They were sad because of the near total destruction caused by the earthquake.

He lay there quietly for some time. Even then, he felt he was trembling from within as he was not able to forget that cracking sound, Gomti's fearful eyes as she tried to sit up and how she was thrown back and finally into the earth.

A Christian nurse gave him a pill and his eyes grew heavy with sleep.

When he woke up, again he had felt the tremors but everything was quiet in a moment. Outside the tent, he heard two people talking, "This time the tremor was very mild . . . . . . what is now left of the village to be destroyed?" He was listening to this conversation sitting in his bed. The pale light of the stars was reflected in the dark night. He could hear the moaning sounds of other injured patients who lay around him. His head still felt heavy from the sleeping pill. Once again he had a vision of Gomti's body on the rocking bed and he got up. Very slowly he slipped out of the tent, unnoticed. The sky looked cloudy outside and he felt a few rain drops. A nurse was asleep in an armchair. There were many other tents, like the one he was in. Several army trucks stood in line in a far corner.

On leaving his tent, he began walking in the direction of the sea. He felt as if the sea was calling him, as he slowly neared the seashore. Gomti had proved her point by disappearing into the bowels of the earth like Sita[1]. But why did she have to prove her truth in this hard way? He could not even remember why she was cross with him that night, nor could he remember the reason that had made her sleep in that corner! All that he remembered was Gomti's sad face, that deafening cracking roar and her disappearance into the earth. He could not recollect anything beyond that. This earthquake had destroyed almost

---

[1] wife of Rama a mythological character of the ancient Indian epic *Ramayana*.

the whole village. He felt like visiting his house once but then he grew afraid, lest somebody should again seize him and make him lie down in the tent. He was not prepared for this now, so he continued walking towards the sea.

He was startled as the cold sea washed his feet. His resolution made in sheer helplessness dissolved as he felt the high tide on his feet, but he continued to walk for quite some time.

As he walked, his decision to commit suicide gave him a chance to think about death — the sea water would slowly run into his lungs and in a breathless state his soul would leave his body, and would all this be easy? The designs made by the insects on the wet sand pricked his bare feet and numbed his consciousness ....

"And, I turned back," said the old man, "Perhaps, if the beach of this coast were not this long, I would have drowned but ......"

Aalok was badly shaken by the story. He did not say anything as he would not have been able to compose himself. The evening had already turned into night and the old man unable to read the expression on Aalok's face, went on, "I continued to live, married a second time but did not stay in the same house. We had children, but fate took them away. My wife has been suffering from filaria for the past two years. I had brought her back from the hospital only a month ago and now, I am waiting for death to arrive and take me away ..." the old man said, rising.

Aalok too got up. They walked some distance in silence. All of a sudden Aalok stopped. He took the old man's hand in his and said, "You will excuse me sir, but I have a query ..."

"Yes?"

"Had Gomti been saved in your place what would she have done? Would she have tried to commit suicide?"

The old man stopped walking. His lips were trembling. The answer which was clear in his eyes came to his lips after a second. "No," he said firmly. "Perhaps she would have gone mad ......"

Far away in the background, the murmur of the waves could be heard like the pathetic laughter of some mad woman, ruffling the darkness of the night.

When Aalok reached his hotel, a petromax lamp glowed outside his room, while inside a maid was changing the bed-sheet in the light of a lantern. He stood on the verandah. The servant who became aware of his presence hurriedly finished her work and came out of the room saying, "Sir, may I lay the table for dinner?"

Christine was nowhere to be seen. The maid came twice to inquire whether he required anything.

Even from a distance, the soft music from Christine's transistor could be heard. This music went on till late in the night. When he went to bed after turning off the petromax, he became aware of some footsteps nearby. It seemed there were more than two persons. They were walking towards Christine's house. The footsteps became faint. Apparently, they had settled on the swing that was outside Christine's house. Christine spoke to them in hushed tones. The voices of the other people were not clear, Aalok could only hear them indistinctly. Within minutes they came back and passed by Aalok's room. Tommy had growled a little and then stopped. Aalok could not sleep. He sat up and tried to read something in the light of the lantern.

F OUR

The noise of the water mill on the well could be heard. Who could be drawing water at this time of the night? He wondered and became thoughtful. The breeze blew and during the whole night, he could hear the sound of water being drawn from the well and being collected in water tanks. He had a feeling that somebody sat continuously near the well. He had no courage to sit up in bed; and so he covered himself upto his head with a bed-sheet and shut his eyes.

"I am sorry, I could not be present last night during dinner," said Christine, while preparing the morning tea. "But did you sleep well? Our water mill was making such a noise last night. The whole night there was a strong wind blowing and now the water tanks are overflowing."

"I have not yet completed a whole day in your village but I can say it appears to be very good ......"

"Yes, the village is nice, but its life has disappeared," said Christine. "What prosperity there was a decade ago! In those days our hotel was always full and to get accommodation was so difficult! People coming from and going to other villages were so keen on staying here that they would not go any further till they first drank our toddy[1]."

Sipping his tea, Aalok listened to Christine.

"In the old days, I would see to it that every customer was comfortable. I would myself inquire about their needs. But once a Parsi[2] couple had come to stay here. I was very young at that time and newly married," said Christine. Aalok looked at Christine, who was talking with her eyes on her cup of tea; but she felt Aalok's gaze. She continued, "After seeing them to their room, as I was going away, I heard the lady say, 'This silly girl likes my husband so much that every five minutes she comes here on some pretext!' I was taken aback. I went to my room and cried my heart out. My husband comforted me and said, 'Our business is such, you should not take these things to heart. If you become so touchy, how can we run the hotel?' But, ever since then, after dusk, I don't go to anybody's room to ask about anything."

Aalok felt like asking her, "Where is your husband now?" but he could not bring himself to do so. Christine would have talked more had not an old Parsi gentleman arrived, and sat on the footsteps.

"How are you Rustomjee?"

"I am fine, madam, I heard that some passenger has come to stay here so I thought of asking him whether he would like to visit the toddy-palm forest in my horse-carriage?"

---

[1] a fermented alcoholic drunk.
[2] a member of the Zorastrian religious set in India, descended from a group of Persian refugee who fled from Muslim persecution in the 7th and 8th century A.D.

"This passenger is not of the kind who would like to see the forest!" said Christine laughingly.

"I would like to go. What else will I do here?" said Aalok.

Rustomjee talked all the way. "Sir, there was a time ...... when twenty-five horse-carriages would be standing outside the Urad Road Station. Then came the transport service. So now, in the whole village, mine is the only carriage left. My children are now calling me to Bombay; but I cannot leave this village. I love this place very much and Burjor's mother, my wife, is suffering from cancer. She may not live for more than a year or two. I don't feel like leaving this place."

The carriage was slowly passing through the toddy-palm estates and he remembered Manjari; perhaps if she had been here with him, she would have gone to see Rustomjee's ailing wife. She would also have tried to lift the veil of blankness in his faded eyes which were seen through the spectacles that rested on his nose. Aalok too would have reacted in the same way. But he was still under the spell of the stunning conversation he had had with the old man at the seashore.

So he asked, "Were you here six decades ago when the earthquake occurred?"

Rustomjee pulled the reins in a reflex action and the carriage stopped. "Yes," he sighed and again the carriage started moving slowly. "I had gone to the nearby village; the tremors of the earthquake were felt there too, but they were very mild and not very damaging, but when I came back here, oh, what I saw ......"

Instead of listening to Rustomjee, Aalok's mind was full of the previous night's encounter with the old man.

"Is Jivobhai there?" Rustomjee asked, stopping the carriage outside a hut.

"No, he has gone out of the village," a woman said coming out of the hut. She was about twenty-five years old and was scantily dressed. She said, "Come in uncle, fresh toddy is ready ......"

Aalok also got down from the carriage. He said, "Have a drink Uncle, but I will not. I am not a regular drinker. I will have some plain water."

"This toddy will not intoxicate you sir," the lady said cleaning the bench for her visitors. "This Rustom Uncle of ours can drink half a drum of toddy at one sitting!"

"Those days have gone now ...," said Rustomjee. "Sir, I've known this Jamna, since she was a child. She used to work at our place, but then Jiva started this business and there was no need for Jamna to work. It was good of the Government to have enforced prohibition ..."

Jamna brought two glasses of toddy and placed them on the bench. Rustomjee drank the whole glass in one draught.

Aalok became thoughtful with the glass in his hand, and after a while slipped the glass into Rustomjee's hands and made a move to go towards the toddy-palm jungle.[1]

"Sir, would you like to see how toddy is tapped?"

Aalok looked at her with a smile. Jamna did not understand the smile but she left the sleepy Rustomjee where he was and went along with Aalok. She showed him a vessel tied to the tree trunk which was being tapped. "When my father returns, he will bring down the vessel, full of toddy."

"Is Jivabhai your father?"

"Yes, who else did you think?"

"I thought he was your ......"

"My husband lives in Saroda, ten miles from here. But I would not allow him to come anywhere near here," said Jamna.

"Why?"

Jamna remained silent.

Aalok looked at Jamna. She was chewing a leaf of the toddy palm. She stopped chewing and said, "Sir, people of our race are like that ......"

"But what happened?"

"Oh, that swine started gambling and he vomitted blood ......", said Jamna.

Aalok could not understand her.

"Sir, among our people, they play this game — gadi."[2]

"What does that mean?"

_____

[1] a palm grove where toddy is tapped.

[2] a sort of superstititious gambling prevalent among the tribals of South Gujarat.

"You see, there are two persons. Between the two, a line is drawn and then both the parties secretly start chanting. Then both parties thrash one another. The one who vomits blood is defeated. My husband started playing. He drank a full drum of toddy, but then he could not bear any more and got defeated. He started abusing me, saying 'You are not a good woman and because I am married to you, I lost the game. All these years I have never been defeated.' As if this were not enough, that rascal friend of his took our hut as well." Jamna's eyes were turbulent. Aalok understood what she wanted to convey.

"I told him, 'Let your bet go to hell. I will go away to my father's place.' I cannot let anybody else touch my body lest my mother goddess becomes angry."[1]

"Then?"

"Ever since, I've been with my father ...... My husband will not give me a divorce and I am not willing to stay with him and run his house. I have stayed with him for two months and have had enough. Now I serve my old father."

When they returned, Rustomjee was lying on the bench.

"It seems the old man has gone to sleep."

"He must be drunk," said Aalok.

"Oh no, even if he drinks the whole drum, nothing would happen to him. Its just that he has dozed off."

It seemed to Aalok that the whole village had dozed off. Leaving the carriage at the outskirts of the village, Aalok slowly walked down towards his hotel. Most of the houses in the village had a swing in their verandahs, where many old Parsi ladies and gents dozed. Elsewhere, some children were playing cricket. But most of the houses were quiet. Though it was noon, there were about fifteen people in the General Library all busy reading the previous day's paper that had arrived by the day's train; two persons were simultaneously reading the same page of the newspaper. It looked like they were determined to read each and every word of it!

When Aalok reached his hotel he saw that Christine had been waiting for him.

23

---

[1] the wrath of the guardian deity.

F<small>IVE</small>

Like an obstinate bullock, the afternoon seemed not to move. Once
again Aalok picked up his pen to write a letter to Manjari.
He changed his mind and put it down as he felt like staying
a few more days in this newly acquired solitude. If he wrote
the letter, he was sure, Manjari would come to him. And then
they would be considered as one of the many young couples.
Everybody would see them that way, behave with them in that
fashion, and once again a world of social customs and courte-
sies would be created. Her parents would send them telegrams
every day, and their motor car would also come, driven by her
cousin; picnics would be arranged on the seashore or in the
toddy-palm jungle.

While he was thinking about Manjari, he remembered Christine and Jamna. Till today he had seen Manjari in Kitty, Mohana,
Sulu, Nilanjana and the like. But how would Manjari look besides Jamna? He had a feeling that till today he had never observed
a woman in the true sense. He was able to appreciate women like
Manjari, Sulu, Nilanjana, or for that matter Christine or Jamna
only superficially. He had observed that Manjari was able to talk
nicely, and was perhaps more capable of listening sympathetically
to others. And he could not dislodge from his mind Nilanjana's
very attractive blue eyes. He also liked the smile that lurked at
the corner of Christine's lips. And Jamna's youthful body seen
through her light clothes was so attractive that he was afraid even
to look! But after all, these beautiful things were superficial. He
was unable to know the real Manjari when she had listened to
him engrossed — he had of course never tried to know her real
self beyond the world of their relationship! And he wondered
what Manjari would gain once she came to his house as a bride
leaving her world full of relatives. Perhaps the reality of existence
is no more present in the blue eyes of Nilanjana; or the emotions she is trying to conceal. Behind the curtain of innocence

is where it probably lies! And, where is the truth of Christine's existence? Her husband? Could he be dead or was it just that he was out of town? Or . . .? And why was Jamna satisfied with her two months of married life? Was the satisfaction of her biological needs fulfilled so easily? Or could it be that she too was deceiving herself?

Perhaps there is only one woman really . . . . . . and it is that presence that lives in Manjari, in Jamna and in Christine at the same time!

Aalok would have continued to ruminate but a knock at the door woke him from his day-dream.

"Madam wants to know whether you would like to join her in her room for tea?" asked Shankar.

That night he was unafraid of the sound of the water mill. He sat on the verandah. The petromax had been extinguished two hours earlier. Now it must be one o'clock in the morning, perhaps two or even three! The sky was turning pale. The elusive morning before the dawn! He remembered one of his school friends saying:

"At night a deceitful morning rises — this morning belongs to the world of spirits and when our morning arrives, they disappear into the air."

As he remembered this, he thought he saw a white figure by the side of the well — he rubbed his eyes. There was nobody near the well. Again that figure became visible when he stared fixedly at it.

He felt like going over, taking a stroll to find out what was there, but then he saw Tommy sleeping at his doorstep and he faltered and thought he would unnecessarily wake all the others.

He tried to identify the stars in the sky. When young, he could recognize many of them, easily identifying one from the other as one would separate known faces from a crowd of unknown ones. This thought pleased him and his loneliness disappeared. For a long time he continued gazing at the stars.

In the morning he had tea with Christine, listened to the cricket commentary on the transistor and then went to the seashore.

Today the old man was not to be seen and the boys also were not playing around. Only the hotel boy Shankar was sleeping on the sand and on seeing him Aalok stopped and went back. And then night fell . . . .

Today, he had not been able meet the doctor about whom Christine had spoken. She had said that the doctor and his wife were the only intelligent people in the whole village and that if he met them, his evening would be very pleasant. But Aalok did not feel like going to see them today. Instead, he wanted to watch a drama as a troupe of actors had arrived in the village. But he dropped that idea too. He became thoughtful instead and began to dissect his own emotions and feelings.

Why did he not go to meet the doctor and his wife and why did he not want to see the drama? He could not understand. He was all alone this evening, spending his time at the seashore, his mind teeming with lonely thoughts.

He remembered his childhood — his early days in Bombay, his first meeting with Manjari! And thought of the station master of Urad Road.

From the very beginning Aalok's life had run smoothly; he had always tried to change it in a new direction — but somehow he never had to face any difficult or adverse situation and so never had to change his set pattern of life. Am I tired of this routine? Aalok wondered.

Perhaps, here, in Urad, he might be able to give a different twist to his life, but would he be able to live in Urad? Aalok felt he was getting involved in a fantasy world. Did he really want to live here all his life? These few days might pass without difficulty — and then, back to the normal routine life! When Aalok saw Chhanalal coming with glowing embers in his hands, he felt like screaming. Chhanalal's face burned red in the glow of the fire. He held the embers in front of him.

"Chhanabhai, how can you do this? You could have burned your face!

"Oh sir, how can one who has already been burnt by the fire of fate, get hurt with coal?" answered Chhanalal.

His face was made up. Only a few minutes earlier, he was on stage and remembering his ballerina, had wept so pathetically that even a stone would have melted. After that, now in the warmth of the furnace, he recalled that unforgettable scene.

Aalok was casually introduced to this simple person. That evening, instead of going towards the sea-shore, he had gone to the place where the mobile drama troupe had camped. As soon as Chhanalal saw him coming, he had got up from his chair, thrown away his half-smoked cigarette and welcomed him respectfully saying, "Come in, Sir."

Aalok could not reject his spontaneous invitation to the play he was to act in and Chhanalal had given him a seat in the wing. Aalok was familiar with the professional and amateur theatre of Bombay and there were people who knew and respected him, but this manager of a very different kind of a mobile drama troupe, intrigued him tremendously. It seemed that in a lifeless world this man was living from within. Perhaps in a lively atmosphere, he would have been a different individual.

"Actually, for some time, I too was in the limelight!" said Chhanalal, "But my fate was not so good and I had to leave everything. Sir, do you remember, in Bombay there was a drama troupe called 'Sudharak Mandali' in Play House?"

Aalok did not remember; But even so, he nodded.

"When the play Ra-Navghan was staged, I played the role of the protagonist Navghan," said Chhanalal. "Vilasvati was the heroine and sir, we were very popular in Bombay. When I sang that song, I used to get more than five to six encores. Without those 'once mores', the curtain would not fall …. Even for the sixty-fifth show I got six encores."

Chhanalal was absorbed in his own thoughts but suddenly he became aware of something: it was time for his entry onto the stage and like a mad man, he ran on, crying for his beloved: "Charanya, where are you, Charanya ..." and he began lamenting his lost beloved who had drowned in the overflowing river. Chhanalal must have been around fifty at that time, and it seemed he performed all the leading roles. His face looked old and pitiable but once on stage, it was as though some powerful spirit entered him, and his face shone.

Aalok thought that the weeping of Chhanalal had an authentic ring. Was he crying for his lost beloved of the stage or was it some soul of a medieval poet which had entered his body? Or was it memories of his past life and loss of fame that made him weep in such a genuine fashion?

As soon as the scene on the stage was over, he returned to Aalok. As Ratan, the actress of the drama, passed by, he stopped her and introduced Aalok saying, "Ratan, this sahib has come from Bombay. He appreciates your acting: just now ... praising you ......"

"Yes, sister, your performance was very good," said Aalok.

Ratan could not follow the language but smiled modestly and went away. Chhanalal stared at Aalok making him curious. He was about to say something when Chhanalal said, "Sir, I thought of something."

"What?"

"Perhaps for the first time in her life, somebody addressed her as 'sister'. I have known her since she was eight years old. Her mother used to work for our drama troupe. Everybody used to call her 'Ratni', then she became Ratanbai — then in the city, nobody took any notice of her and she was discarded. Since then she has been working for drama troupes like ours, where she is either addressed as Ratan or bai[1]."

For Aalok, this was a whole new world. A girl who had never been addressed as a daughter or a sister since her birth, a woman who had perhaps never had a childhood — described in contexts like, "She will drive many men crazy when she grows up," or "She is just like her mother" and so her childhood passes

---

[1] a respectful form of addressing Maharashtrian women.

by — she has only one reference in life, youth; and it could be her past youth or what lies ahead.

Chhanalal continued his story and said, "Sir, I was in love with Vilas — once I told her so and she told me, 'Don't pretend', and I said to her, 'Silly thing, had I known how to act, what more would I have desired?' "

Aalok felt that Chhanalal was talking about some perrennial secret which he himself did not understand. Truth could be hidden; but if one wanted to openly tell the truth, one had to act, and very few people have the courage to act like that!

"Sir, our director did not approve of our being in love. He used to say, 'He who falls in love with his heroine, loses the art of acting' and so he not only dismissed me but disgraced me so much that no drama company was prepared to hire me. Actually, he was afraid that if we got married, we would start a drama company of our own ......"

Chhanalal removed the ashes from the furnace and from his face, saying, "It was then that I formed this drama troupe, and earned enough to support myself and the others who are dependant on me. Sometimes when we meet people like you, our life gets a push or two."

The play was over. After the fourth cup of tea with Chhanalal, Aalok tried to put a tenner into the actor's pocket before leaving. But Chhanalal was startled by his gesture and said, "No sir, when people like you visit our place, it becomes a sacred event, and we consider it our good fortune".

When Aalok came out, the moon was high in the sky. At a distance, in the jungle of toddy-palm trees, some celebration was going on. He could hear the strident strains of music. Most viewers of the audience had dispersed but a few were standing near a mobile tea stall.

When Aalok walked along the moonlit road, he remembered Chhanalal's words, 'Sir, once I was famous ......" How many deaths this one man had died during his lifetime! He had ceased to be a hero, he had lost his fame, he hadn't get Vilas — his beloved; his love had died. He was still living! At the age of fifty, he was doing the role of a lover — his eyes, full of madness, cast a magical spell on stage: Chhanalal was perhaps the truth of the stage; he was everything in that atmosphere, but removed from that atmosphere he was nobody.

Seven

"You are very late? Will you have something to drink?" asked Christine who was reading in the light of the petromax[1] in the verandah. She got up when she saw Aalok.

Instead of going towards his room, Aalok sat on the verandah of Christine's room. Christine was in a green, embroidered night-gown. Her face, always gloomy was even more so tonight. This gloom accentuated her age as well as her beauty. Her hair was a little dishevelled.

"What will you have? Something cold or hot?" asked Christine.

"Whatever you have."

"Will you join me in whatever I drink?" asked Christine.

Aalok was startled, but very coolly he replied, "Yes, I will drink whatever you have."

Christine went inside and called Aalok in after her. His eyes had to get used to the darkness of the room as Aalok entered the room from the dazzling light of the petromax. Inside the room were two lanterns and their light reminded him of the moonlight that had bathed him on the road.

Christine opened the wine cellar. She took out a bottle on which was written 1868 ......

"This is a present from my grandfather. Will you have some?"

"Christine, I will only have a soft drink, but you can go ahead."

"Are you averse to drinking?"

---

[1] a kerosene lamp which emanates light and used by affluent villagers where electricity is not available.

"No, but I am not habituated; and I don't think I have time enough left in life to form new habits ......"

"Why do you say that? You have hardly knocked at life's door and you have still to enter its arena."

"Well, do we know whether the door by which we are standing, will take us into life or out of life when it opens?" said Aalok.

"You speak in riddles. I cannot understand," said Christine, "I will not force you. Please sit down, I will be back in a minute ......"

Aalok sat outside on the verandah. He was unable to understand Christine. Though she ran a hotel, she was a different type of woman. Perhaps, she was also an outsider to this environment. Who could have planted her roots here?

That chain of thought was broken when Christine put the glasses on the table. Seeing his startled look, Christine said laughingly, "Don't worry, I will not convert you. Your glass contains nothing but a soft drink, and of course, what I have in my glass is also known as a woman's drink ......"

Christine sat opposite him. Her eyes were the only part of her body that shone and showed some life. Very slowly she took a sip from the glass and continued to gaze into the glass. The light red liquid in the glass showed pink in the light of the petromax. For a long time she went on playing with the glass in her hand while Aalok talked about the play he had seen and about Chhanalal whom he had met.

"How quickly you finished your drink!" Christine said preparing another glass for him while taking another sip from hers. Suddenly she became silent. Aalok felt the heaviness of her silence. One moment he would look at Christine and the next moment at the glass in his hand.

"Don't you feel like asking me, Aalok, why at this hour of the night, almost after midnight, I sit with a drink in hand and what sort of a woman I am, drinking in the presence of a stranger?" Christine said in one breath.

Aalok smiled bleakly then said, "I will not lie, I am curious to know about you, and I am not in two minds regarding what sort of a woman you are. I may not know who you are, but I am very clear in my mind as to what you are."

"What am I?"

"You are a fine woman. Any chaste woman can feel jealous about your being nice, attractive and pious," said Aalok "and I am not just saying this. Today the woman who drinks with me, after midnight, is perhaps passing through the most painful moments in her life. I am sorry, Christine, it is not polite for any respectable man to take an interest in another's personal life — but this wine does not intoxicate — it only enhances the sadness of the transparently gloomy atmosphere that surrounds you. The transparency decreases and among the layers of the sadness your face is becoming more and more foggy. I wonder who has the power to penetrate these layers of sadness?"

Christine smiled, trying to shake off the seriousness and then she said, "You used the word 'pious' for me, didn't you?"

"Why? Yes . . . ."

"You were afraid that I might become unholy, and you used that word to warn me?"

"Christine, at midnight, to sit and drink wine in the presence of a stranger, who does not drink, demands a lot of trust in that person. Your nerves are a bit excited because of the wine but I am absolutely calm. At this moment, I cannot fear you, if at all anybody should feel fear, it should be you."

"You talk as if we are demons trying to eat each other! . . . . . . forget it . . . . I was trying to tell you something else. I really wondered why during all these days you have never asked me a single question about myself. Other customers have tried to find out on their first day as to why I live alone, where my husband is, how many children I have and so forth — you are so different from others — perhaps that is why I could trust you."

The word trust put Aalok on his guard. The alcohol was slowly working on Christine, stimulating her and though she was absolutely under control, she became loquacious.

"Aalok, sometimes I wonder why I continue to live. Sometimes we are left alone at crossroads and it becomes difficult to find the beginning or the end of the road and know the directions. It does not matter which way we turn and in which direction we go, the result will be the same. We come back to the point from where we set out, and that makes us feel so childish and stupid, it takes away our courage to start the journey all over again; or sometimes we reach a dead end ......"

While Christine spoke, Aalok stared at the long shadows that were on the outside pavement as the light of the petromax flickered.

"Christine," said Aalok, "it is very late and you must be tired."

"Yes, Aalok, it is late and I am tired, and I will not be fresh in the morning. When I wake up in the morning, I'm more tired than ever; I'm afraid. I am afraid my husband will return: when the last train at night passes by, I feel my worries are over for the day and I sleep without fear."

"Your husband ...... what is the harm if he returns?"

"He is overfond of me — and I cannot see him unhappy. The sight of me makes him extremely unhappy. For the past eight years he has not come here. I do not even know his whereabouts. Whenever he sends a money order or a draft say after six or eight months, I would know from where he has sent that. Sometimes it even comes from some foreign country! Many a time I have wondered as to where he is. Would he have remarried? He had a very unsteady mind. The mother of this boy Shankar, also used to work here, and well, I do not know why but I see a great resemblance between my husband and Shankar. May be I am mistaken, I have never asked him; but I am sure he must have married again. He cannot get through a single night without a woman."

"But he has stayed for eight years without you! What about that?" Aalok could not refrain from asking.

"Aalok," said Christine, "I told you that he does not come here because he loves me too much."

Aalok could not understand anything. He was bewildered and stared at Christine. She gulped down the remaining drink left in her glass and putting it down on the table said, "It is very late and you must be feeling sleepy ..."

Aalok got up unwillingly: Their talk too had ended abruptly like Christine's shadow. But it was possible that if their talks had continued, Christine would have been even more hurt. Aalok went out.

"Aalok ...," she called again.

Aalok turned and went back to where Christine still stood.

"Aalok, I do not know why, but today, I want to tell you everything. Since you have told me about trust, the great trust a woman who drinks must have in a man who does not indulge and who is sober! When I have such trust in you, I thought why not unburden myself and tell you a small detail? When everybody asked me why my husband does not come here, I lied to them. But you are the only one who has not asked me anything, and so I want to give you the truth," said Christine and swiftly unzipped her night gown letting it fall off her shoulders ... Aalok suppressed a scream at what he saw and closed his eyes with his hands.

"This is unbearable, Christine."

"You are unhappy just looking at it, while he was supposed to desire it; and he loved me. The initial small patch of leucoderma that was in the middle of my chest increased to such an extent! Nature has stamped ugliness on my beauty in such a way that nobody in the world can see it. And as I said, my husband is a very unstable person, and though he stayed married to me, could not enjoy me and endure me. For a long while after marriage, he stayed with me but was very unhappy. Then he started this hotel. He would come here. He would look very jovial and happy and I would always pray the night would not fall. Inevitably night it would be. He would come to me, try to take me in his arms but could never embrace me, as he would remember that ugly patch. He would say, 'When I see this patch, I just melt from within as if I have suddenly reached the sun ...' and he would become sad. I would prepare a champagne cocktail so we could forget the agony, but instead, our unhappiness would deepen. Then he started coming once a month or so and after sometime he stopped visiting altogether. Neither of us ever said anything to the other — but we both knew and understood; and sometimes I still wonder where he must be. Is he happy?"

Christine stopped talking. She had become breathless and Aalok did not know what to say; his lips had become dry and his whole body stiff. Christine laughed and said, "I am very sorry, Aalok, after a certain moment has passed one feels how good it would have been, had that moment not arrived at all.

And just now I feel like that. I feel, how it would have been had we not sat here like this tonight? I would not have been put into this predicament and now I will not be able to raise my head."

Aalok thought he should say something, but he could not utter a word. His mind had gone blank. He turned silently and went into his room. The moon had risen high but Aalok could not glance at it. He remembered the moon that was on Christine's chest. He hurried to his own room as if to save himself. Entering his room, he shut the door and went to bed.

Sleep seemed to elude him. He passed the rest of the night in a half wakeful state all the while aware that there was some sort of sound from Christine's room. But before he could decide whether all this was a dream or reality, his eyes closed.

Eight

It was nine o'clock in the morning when Aalok woke up. He became perplexed and at once got out of bed; only to realise where he was, and the easy pace of life in this place. It could be either nine in the morning or nine at night. He then recollected the happenings of the previous night; the talk and the subsequent events; was it all a nightmare? The play; Chhanalal with the burning furnace in his hands; Christine, moving her hand with a glassful of wine; her standing on the verandah with that unforgettable white wound on her breast . . . . . .

He brushed his teeth and sat leaning against the cot. He did not feel like going out on to the verandah to have his morning tea. Instead, when Shankar called him, he requested him to bring the tea in.

At lunch time, Aalok felt a sense of relief when he did not see Christine. In fact, Aalok had mentally rehearsed so many different sentences in order to start a conversation with Christine, if he should happen to encounter her; but would he really be able to say anything to her?

That he had silently walked out of the room last night, weighed heavily on Aalok's mind. He should have said something, if only a few words to console Christine. Had he really tried, he would have found the words, but his mind had gone blank.

Now he was able to look back at the whole event in its right perspective. Last night he had felt sorry for Christine's husband, but he was also touched by Christine's agony; now he felt that the veil of sadness that had been built around Christine's face was beyond reach and perception. She was a wonderful woman — the beauty of her veiled body and the ugliness of her unveiled figure: perhaps reality existed in neither state. Aalok felt that to differentiate between beauty and ugliness was futile. Christine had her own unique beauty — a beauty that was as sad and as transparent as the atmosphere in which she lived. Her husband had never discovered that beauty; but had he been able to perceive and reach the beauty of her inner self, surely he would not have been so aloof and distant from her for so long a period!

But had not Christine said, "When the sight of this patch is unbearable to you, what about the man who was supposed to desire me!" Isn't there more to life than the physical enjoyment that a man can get from a woman!

And why is it that this simple fact had not dawned on Christine? What would happen if he were to become disfigured after marrying Manjari? The thought made him shiver. In intimate moments with Manjari, he had taken her close and embraced her. But he had never seen her unwrapped beauty; not that he did not wish to see it, but somehow he had not felt like looking at the hidden beauty of a young woman before marriage. That was why he could sit with Manjari for hours together without getting involved.

Suppose he had run away like Christine's unsteady husband, what would Manjari have done? Like Christine, would she have lived alone dreaming? Such a natural thing for a woman to do! She manages to live with a smiling face after her passions are spent! How much suffering had she undergone in order to face the world normally? Now he could imagine the pressures under which Christine was able to keep a smiling face!

In the afternoon too, Shankar brought his tea into the room.

"What is Madam doing?" Aalok inquired.

"She is asleep. Shall I wake her?" asked Shankar.

"No," said Aalok.

Nine

Christine was right.

Aalok, though he had not been introduced to Dr. Meherwan and Piloo, would never have believed that such an intelligent couple could live in a place like Urad. When they met for the first time, Piloo at once recognised him and had said: "You are Aalok, aren't you? Meherwan, he is the person Christine was telling us about."

"Welcome," said Meherwan. "Had you not come today, we would have come to meet you. Christine has told us so much about you!"

"I'd be happy only if I could prove to be even a little like the picture she has drawn of me," said Aalok, looking at the drawing hung on the wall. It had a picture of an iceberg floating in the sea and on that iceberg stood a man. He felt that he had seen it before.

"You must have seen this picture in the *Life* magazine. In my leisure hours I have tried to copy it," said Meherwan.

Now Aalok remembered this picture and its context; and said: "You have done this picture differently from the original photo …"

"I liked it very much — it shows the true concept of ourselves. The man is standing on an iceberg which he knows is melting every moment and is deliberately waiting for that moment when he will be drown …."

"Do you draw?" asked Meherwan.

"Not as well as a professional artist; but when it becomes a compulsion, I do scrawl a few lines here and there!"

"But tell me, how have you lived in this town for so many days?" asked Piloo.

"I now feel I can live here for the rest of my life!" said Aalok. But the heaviness in his voice betrayed his untruthful words. He knew he would never be able to live here his whole life; did he really know what life meant? He was simply saying the words for the sake of their beautiful sounds!

Meherwan said, "It all depends on the life one has!"

Aalok felt these words of Meherwan had uncovered the veil of untruths. Aalok felt slightly embarrassed.

He said, "Yes, sometimes we tend to say that the mirage seen on the road is real. Actually, we hardly live life at all!"

"Aalok, you have touched a very serious topic. I think you and Piloo can continue talking. I have an important visit to make. A child had a fever of 104 degrees this afternoon and I had to give him an injection and some medicines. I told them that I would call on them in the evening. I shall return in no time," Meherwan said, as he put on his jacket. He collected his emergency bag and left.

Aalok observed the interior decor of the doctor's house. Hardly any furniture, but what little there was, was beautiful. On the table there was a photograph of a small child. Next to the table, there were rows of plays and novels on shelves.

"Who is interested in these books? You? Or the Doctor?" asked Aalok.

"If I have to name only one person, then it is Meherwan who reads them. I too read a few books suggested by him," said Piloo.

"Are there enough patients in this town for him to treat?"

"We always pray that, there should not be too many patients, that people should remain healthy — but somehow, the number of patients has never decreased."

Aalok got up and started looking at the wall which was covered with pictures and certificates, the Doctor's certificates, a group photo at the hospital in Bombay and so on ...

"Were you in Bombay before you came here?"

"Yes."

"Why did you settle down here?"

Piloo was silent and grew serious as she looked out of the window. Then suddenly she called the servant and asked for tea.

"This whole village is sick," said Aalok."Perhaps only a doctor like Meherwan can diagnose what is wrong and treat it, but its pulse is fading and I feel, some day it is going to die a natural death."

"You sound very pessimistic, or else you have not seen this village at all," said Piloo. "Here we do not get that impatient, we do not hurry and live the way city people do. In the city, man runs fast in the direction of death, while here, we live perhaps a fuller life without any anxiety."

Aalok remained silent. He did not feel like answering her. It was like building a bridge in an unfamiliar valley where the bridge crumbled before he could finish it. He could have talked about many other topics but he felt that this was not the time for it.

"Your tea is getting cold."

And all of a sudden Aalok was brought back to reality from his day dream.

"What were you thinking of so intently?"

"Oh no, nothing much. I was just thinking that I should make a move now. It looks as if Doctor may be delayed."

"Perhaps he is on his way back" said Piloo, and at that very moment the maid servant entered the house.

"Doctor has sent a message that he is delayed. Kishore's temperature is a 106 degrees. He has requested the guest to wait till he returns," the maid said.

Piloo's face reflected sorrow and anxiety. She asked the maid, "Is there any ice available?"

"Yes, they got it from the Christian boarding house," said the maid and went away.

"Who is this Kishore?"

"He's a nice boy; and loves to visit the dispensary morning and evening. We too have grown attached to him and feel anxious if he does not come. He has been ill the past two days and we are very worried about his condition," said Piloo.

Aalok stared at the photograph of a child which was on the table. Piloo observed this and became tense. Her lips trembled a little but she did not speak.

"The world of children — it is a unique one, isn't it? I too like children very much. It is only with a child that one can laugh freely."

Piloo did not say anything; and Aalok did not know how to keep the conversation going. The heaviness on Piloo's face became more pronounced.

"You look very anxious. You are worried about Kishore, are you?"

"Yes, I suppose so."

"I have faith in our Doctor, the mere touch of his hands will cure Kishore ......"

Two drops of tears fell from Piloo's eyes. Aalok was stunned to see tears coursing down her cheeks.

"Excuse me," Piloo said getting up. She went into the inner room and came back after washing her face.

"Your words had a nostalgic effect and I remembered something from my past ......"

"It seems I have touched a sensitive spot. Have I hurt you?"

"No, but once I too said exactly what you said just now."

"When?"

"When my son was ill," said Piloo.

And before Piloo's eyes floated a vision of the face of a small child, Shyavaksha....

Shyavaksha was a handsome little boy. He had inherited his parents' features, but nobody had ever imagined he would be such a delicate child. They realised this when he started crawling at seven months. Once he fell down while crawling and cried bitterly as though he had suffered a grievous injury. Then his leg had begun to swell. Piloo's mother had been frightened. Meherwan was on duty in the hospital at that time, so the child was taken there and the x-ray of the leg had shown a fracture. At that time Dr. Shah had diagnosed the case as the "marble bone" disease. Meherwan and Piloo had taken the child to Geneva for treatment. Dr. Brown had kept him in his clinic for three months, during which period he had six new fractures. If the child got excited and ran towards any object or in response to a call from a friend, he was likely to stumble, fall and fracture yet another bone. Unlike other children of his age group he could not run or jump and the parents were unable to bear his helplessness and agony.

Piloo was an optimist. But Meherwan could see the child's future like a movie on the screen: as a doctor Meherwan knew the course the disease would take and in time the child would become lonely; even if he went to school he would not be able to mix with other children; he would fracture his bones every time he tried to walk rapidly. Gradually, all those fractures would cripple him and make him bedridden. He would see others dancing but he himself would never be able to dance; he would be able to listen to music but would never be able to sing freely; and then gradually he would lose his eyesight. There would come a time when he would not be able to see at all; one by one, sparks of life would be extinguished; but there would not be a quick resolution. It would take time for the fire to die out: and then one day. ...

This possible scenario made Meherwan shiver. He never talked to Piloo about it. Piloo always used to say: "Meherwan, you are famed for your healing touch. Your hands will make my Shyavaksha well again ......" Piloo's faith in Meherwan frightened him and so, in spite of his being aware of the truth, Meherwan had not found the courage to stamp out her faith in him.

Dr. Brown had already told them. "There are hardly two or four cases like this in the world and no treatment has been found. As far as possible the patient has to be treated by regular blood transfusion and vitamins; which should be all right for the time being."

Meherwan had not felt like returning immediately to India. So they had stayed in a small French town in the valley of the Alps. It was the month of May and travellers from all over the world visited the place, but the village Meherwan had chosen for them was comparatively quiet.

From the window of their warm hotel room, the snow-clad peaks of the Alps were visible. Shyavaksha would sit in the chair, specially made for him and gaze at the beautiful white mountains. He had now forgotten what it was like to play and be mischievous. He would get up only when somebody called him. Piloo or Meherwan would support him upto the dining table holding his arms. Only then would he walk. His whole body ached but he never complained. Perhaps the small child had taken for granted that life itself was pain!

"In between, he had a bout of cold and fever for two days—but he recovered."

Once on a very pleasant evening, Shyavaksha was sitting in his chair, while Piloo lay on her stomach on the floor with Meherwan by her side. They were admiring the peaks of the Alps.

"Papa!" Shyavaksha began.

"Yes!"

"Can we go over those mountains?"

"Yes!"

"Can I climb?"

"Yes, and when you feel tired, I will carry you."

"Papa, if only I could fly!"

Meherwan looked at Shyavaksha. His fascinated gaze was focused steadily on the highest peak of the mountain ranges that stood in a row, and could be seen through the glass window.

"Then there won't be any question of falling down and breaking any bones, would there?"

"Shyavaksha, we will pass through that row of mountains when we fly over them!"

"Oh, no ... that won't be fun. I want to fly alone: then I will sit on the top of that mountain and call you from there and you will try to find me and look for me here while I will be there, on the top, laughing and looking at you ...!"

Piloo said laughingly, "But we will find you. We will walk up there and bring you back here."

"No, I will detain you there. What will I find there, Papa?"

"Snow."

"Like the one in our fridge?"

"No, this ice is like cotton-wool—it is as soft and as white. But it accumulates slowly and becomes as hard as stone."

"No, papa, there has to be something else too!"

"Like what, son?"

"I will tell you, after I have gone there."

Two or three days after this incident, Meherwan and Piloo were drinking coffee in the ballroom when a message was brought that they were urgently required in their room.

Meherwan and Piloo went up at once. Shyavaksha was lying on the bed and his frightened ayah[1] seated next to him, said to them, "Just see, what has happened to the child!"

Piloo ran to embrace him. Meherwan separated Piloo from the child and taking Shyavaksha's hand in his, checked his pulse; then placed the stethoscope on the child's chest and examined his eyes. He placed his hand across the child's forehead and examined the soles of Shyavaksha's feet. Meherwan grew serious and felt his eyes fill with hot tears.

"Shyavaksha!" said Piloo and again embraced the child.

"Piloo ......" with a suffocating voice Meherwan said, "Shyavaksha is not here."

Piloo stared at Meherwan with vacant eyes.

For sometime Meherwan did not say anything, then he pointed towards the snow-clad mountains and said, "He has flown over there, now we will have to walk up to meet him ......"

Aalok stared unseeingly. He felt as if the photograph of Shyavaksha had grown so large that it covered the whole sky; and then he saw two large tear drops trickling down and rushing as if they were about to destroy the whole universe ... and then the photograph suddenly disappeared, changing the atmosphere in a moment, bringing him back to normal.

Ten

Piloo too had become absorbed in her thoughts when there was a knock on the door. Meherwan entered the house. He was humming a tune. His eyes showed a glow of happiness. Meherwan's presence in the room lifted the veil of gloom.

Piloo wiped her tears and Aalok folded his kerchief. But Meherwan was so engrossed in his own happiness that he did not notice anything. Putting down his bag, he said, "I am

---

[1] a maid servant.

sorry, Aalok, I made you wait so long, but the child has been saved."

"Is Kishore all right?" asked Piloo.

"Yes — now the fever has dropped to a 102 degrees; it will slowly settle, though I was very anxious for the first half hour ......"

"God's grace!" said Piloo and prostrated in front of the photograph of Zarathushtra.[1]

Aalok had coffee with Meherwan. They chatted for an hour; but even so the heaviness he had felt after Piloo's talk did not diminish. During the whole time that they were together, Piloo spoke very little. Meherwan at once guessed that there must have been some reference to Shyavaksha in his absence. So he said, "Aalok, I sometimes really wonder what Shyavaksha will show us on the top of that mountain when we reach there? I am sure there is something more than mere snow over there. But at present our only solace is this small town ... here, during the last three years, I have seen to it that no child has suffered nor a single case failed. Perhaps it is the grace of Shyavaksha, he did not live but I can see him in the lives of all these children. Piloo sometimes cries. I cannot cry. We both would have been crying had Shyavaksha lived. He could have become blind and a cripple and helplessly dependent on us, and how much more painful it would have been for all of us ......!"

It was a dark night and the moon had not risen. Aalok, while walking suddenly stopped.... What made him stop? Where was he going? Doctor and Piloo had an ideal before them, a sure destination. They wanted to go to the top of those mountains. But where did he want to go?

He opened the gate of the boarding house. The light was on in Christine's room, but not in her verandah. His own verandah was lit. He opened his room when Shankar came inquiring, "Saheb, may I bring you dinner?"

"No, I am not hungry," said Aalok.

After sometime there was a knock on his door and Shankar entered with a glass of milk and a dish of biscuits. "Madam requests you to please accept this."

---

[1] founder prophet of the Parsi religion.

Silently Aalok took the glass of milk and Shankar went out closing the door.

In the morning when Aalok went to the breakfast table, Christine met him there. Her hair was wet and hung carelessly, her eyes were red with sleeplessness, but as always she was smiling.

"What are you upto, Aalok?"

"Why? What happened?"

"Yesterday afternoon you did not eat properly. The biscuits I sent with Shankar last night were also returned untouched ... what will our people here think of me if you behave like this in an unknown place and lose weight fasting like this?"

Today, there was a different tone in Christine's voice. The tone was so familiar he felt he'd heard it all his life.

Shankar came with tea and the breakfast tray.

"Today, I woke up early in the morning and prepared the breakfast for you — so, you have to finish it all," said Christine.

Aalok stared at the breakfast plates.

"Am I supposed to eat all this?"

"Yes, you have not eaten since yesterday morning. This is nothing, even a small boy can eat that much."

Silently Aalok began to eat. Christine had prepared tea. She put two teaspoons of sugar into the tea cup — then took the third spoon — "I am making the tea a little more sweet. Perhaps you will find it tasteless after the pudding."

"Well, whatever you give me just now, I have no alternative but to eat quietly."

He was drinking his tea after breakfast when he remembered where he had heard Christine's tone before: that tone was his mother's voice, his aunty's, Manjari's grandma's, Manjari's voice! Perhaps this was the tone of a woman, an affectionate woman!

"What are you thinking?"

"Want me to tell you the truth? Well, at this moment I was thinking of my mother," said Aalok.

Christine gave him a sweet smile and poured some more tea into the cup.

"When are you leaving?" she asked.

"Why? Are you tired of me?"

"No, but I can only arrange my programme after I know the date of your departure ......"

"What is it?"

"I have to go out of town, but how can I, so long as you are here?"

"Christine, are you telling me the truth?"

"Yes!"

"Where are you going?"

"I am going to Daman. I have to visit the church there. Every month or two I go there for confession."

"What will you confess?"

Aalok realised his mistake in asking such a personal question and regretted it instantly.

Christine became serious for a moment but then she laughed, and said, "When I go to Father Valant, I tell him everything that comes to my mind. I never think beforehand ......"

"I may leave tomorrow or the day after; I may decide to go to Daman along with you ......"

"Why?"

"No particular reason. I feel one should certainly visit Daman, having visited this town, but I feel, I will not go along with you."

"Why this sudden change of mind?" said Christine.

"You are going on a pilgrimage, while mine will be a pleasure trip," said Aalok.

For sometime, Christine continued to stare at Aalok. While arranging the cups and saucers on the tray she said, "Aalok, I am reminded of the sermon Father Valant delivered last Christmas: he too used the same two words. Pilgrimage and pleasure trip. He had said 'Many pilgrimages are like pleasure trips; while many a pleasure trip is more sacred than pilgrimages'. But this apart, I am really relieved and feel at peace knowing that you won't be accompanying me."

For sometime, Aalok was silent. Then he said, "When do you propose to go? I think I should now get back to Bombay. It has been a long time since I came and you have not prepared any bill ...."

"Well, I did not mean that you should go just now. Such a small matter and you have taken it to heart ......" said Christine. "Come on now, get ready after a bath. I have called for the carriage. We are going to the temple of Ma Bhawani."

"Temple? Do you believe in that?"

"I know that you believe. And it is said that if a person goes away from this town without visiting the Ma Bhawani temple,[1] then he has to return for her 'darshan'.[2]" said Christine.

"Then, I would like to come again," Aalok said.

The wheels of the carriage were getting stuck in the fine sand on the road. Rustomji was talking about the letter he had received from his son in Bombay. Christine was silently observing the vast sandbed of the sea and the jungle of toddy-palm trees beyond. Aalok was listening to Rustomji's account of his son's letter and nodding in consent, but his mind was on the beautiful atmosphere of the surrounding area.

It was as if the whole atmosphere had changed! Till now he had felt he was imprisoned and suffocating. Now, suddenly, he felt free. The carriage halted under a tree, where there was a small shed and a waterpot underneath.

"Please come, madam," a woman said coming out of the hut, "Have you brought the guest for darshan?"

"Yes", Christine said, smiling at Aalok. "This morning he was reminded of his mother, so I thought it best to bring him here to the Mother Goddess."

They both removed their sandals, washed their feet and drank water. Then both of them went into the temple which was small, with a narrow balcony around its dome. At the back of the temple, lay the sea.

"You please have the 'darshan'; I shall sit on the terrace ......" said Christine.

Christine went on to the terrace and stood there smoothening her wind tossed hair with one hand. It was windy up there and the setting sun cast her shadow so far that it lengthened in front of her upto the beach. "Had the sun been a little lower, the shadow would have reached the sea," she thought. The

---

[1] the spouse of Lord Shiva.

[2] a view or glimpse of God.

green of the sea was reflected in her eyes. This beach was quite different from the one at Urad. Here cyprus trees were few and far between, standing and staring at each other as if they were there by mistake!

Aalok came up, but Christine did not notice him. For sometime, Aalok stood looking at her. What was it in this woman that every time he came near her, he was cast into a different mood? He had almost forgotten Manjari. He behaved as if he never intended to return to city life. When he went very close to her, Christine was startled and held his hand, "Aalok, how different this sea looks now."

Aalok looked deep into Christine's eyes. For a second, she felt strange, then an anxiety and fear gripped her. Slowly she let go of Aalok's hand and said, "I wanted you to see the sea."

"I was looking at the sea through your eyes," said Aalok. "I am talking like a honeymooner, am I not? That too with a woman whom I do not really know?"

The expression on Aalok's face was stranger than usual and Christine was worried about it.

"Do not worry, Christine, I am trying to find out whether my feelings for you are true or false!"

"What feelings?" asked Christine.

"I feel I should stay here forever and not go back ... that I should sit with you on the verandah late into the night and listen to you, that the veil of wonderment that surrounds you should become deeper and that I should just sit there wondering, but without piercing it."

"I am afraid, Aalok," Christine spoke inadvertently. "Do you know what you are talking about?"

"Yes," said Aalok, "and your fear is not baseless. You do not know anything about me, Christine, and I know so much about you! You do not know what is behind my mask of hypocrisy; even I am not aware of it. I am too afraid to remove it."

"Shall we make a move, Aalok? It is almost noon."

"Please sit for sometime Christine, let me finish what I have to say. Have I ever told you about Manjari? Perhaps by now I might have married her; but today I feel, it would have been a grave mistake! I am not the type of person who could belong to her way of life and her kind of circle."

"Aalok, is it that urgent now to decide to which circle you belong? Come, you can think of it on the way back."

While returning, again the carriage had to pass along the sandy road and in the afternoon rays of the sun, it looked as if the sand pillars were standing far away in the distance. Christine at once knew from the expression in Aalok's eyes the anxiety he felt and she inquired, "Aalok, have you ever seen a mirage?"

"No."

"Then look! That is a mirage ......"

ELEVEN

When he thought about Chhanalal, Aalok always felt that the man lived in the past and acted in the present. Just now he was engrossed in his past. They were walking under the shadows of the toddy-palm trees which became longer as the afternoon approached. Suddenly he felt as if some ghost was walking beside him, and he was disturbed at the thought!

The sound of low tide could be heard from a distance away but it seemed Chhanalal was engrossed in hearing the ebbing sound of some other low tide. His eyes held a sparkle and suddenly he stopped walking.

"Sir, we are Targala by caste; we are by profession dancers, singers and actors. We are born with these arts, but now, I do not enjoy performing them. When I cannot enjoy being Chhanalal — myself — how can I enjoy acting, to become Malavpati Munj and do justice to that role?"

Aalok said, "Chhanalal, how can you know which moment you are yourself and which you are Malavpati Munj? I have seen you one moment talking to me backstage as Chhanalal and the next moment on stage when it is your turn, you get so completely engrossed in your role ......"

"Yes sir, when I am Chhanalal, I am Malavpati Munj too. The moment I cease to become Chhanalal I forget the lines of Malavpati Munj as well. Now, when I am talking to you, I do not remember a single word in the dialogue or any sequence of that drama which was once a hit in Bombay. The applause was deafening, and the reason was simple; at that time I was Chhanalal, today I am not ...."

"You mean to say that at present you don't remember a single word of the dialogue of any play that you have performed?"

"No, sir, you will not believe it but have you ever heard the name of that famous actor Chandan Marvadi?"

"Yes, but I haven't had the occasion to see him on stage."

"This Chandan Marvadi was alive only because of alcohol, the very same drink that killed him. He would invariably get drunk. Once it so happened that accidentally some tea spilled on his clothes. He told me, 'Chhanalal, I do not mind this, the tea spilling on my clothes; what I fear very much is that nobody will believe that my clothes were soiled in an innocent accident like a splash of tea. Everybody will say that Chandan must have been lying drunk, in some gutter — and thus soiled his clothes'."

Aalok continued to listen.

"I am sorry, I lost track of things sir, but this Chandan could be himself only when drunk, and only then would he be able to act. When completely drunk, he is hardly conscious. He could not stand erect, but at that time, if he was made up and pushed on stage from the wings, the whole audience would give his entry a standing ovation. This sound would rouse him and he would instantly remember the part he was supposed to play and sir, whatever he spoke in that moment would be really dramatic. Depending on the way he spoke at that time, poets and writers would change their scripts accordingly ......"

Listening to Chhanalal, Aalok felt as though he was on a different plane; as if he himself was on the stage, and had forgotten his dialogue and might perhaps regain his memory only if somebody clapped: and so he looked around him. Rays of the sun could be seen through the leaves of toddy-palm trees as if being sieved through them. Chhanalal tried to light his cigarette which kept going off. Yet Aalok could not remember his dialogue! Chhanalal was right. At present he had ceased to be Aalok and so he was not able to perform his part in the drama of life; a person has to be truthful to perform the right drama.

"You have become deeply thoughtful," said Chhanalal. They had now arrived near the den of Jeeva Kalal. Jamna was drying clothes on the line strung between two trees and she looked at Aalok with a smile of recognition.

"Please step in, sir, you have come after a long time; my father is at home today. Chhanabhai, you too please come ..."

Jeeva came out of the hut.

"Who is it? Chhanabhai?" he asked extending his arm.

"Yes, father, and along with him is the guest who had come the other day ......"

"Please come in, sir, please sit here." Jeeva invited them and started dusting the bench with the cloth that was slung across his shoulders. "What will you have?"

"Jeevabhai, prepare two cups of tea...."

"Do you mean to say that the guests of Jeeva Kalal will drink tea? The times have changed! I am sure you will not mind a real drink, Chhanabhai?"

"No, not today."

"You please go ahead, Chhanabhai. Do not hesitate because of my presence. I have no prejudice against toddy or wine."

"Sir, as it is, we sin so much, but in the presence of a person like you how can I sin by drinking toddy?"

Aalok had a very good answer to this query but felt it would have been beyond Chhanalal's understanding. Instead of confusing him more, Aalok thought it better to keep quiet.

"Sir, my heart is no longer in this town. I feel like going away, somewhere .... but then, what would become of my daughter? Because she is here, she is able to pass her days ...." said Jeeva Kalal.

"You do not like it here?" asked Aalok.

"Sir, the world has changed. Now you hardly come across any large-hearted people. In the past people used to drink to forget the world. Today, they drink to deceive others, those other drinkers are no more. Once upon a time a crowd of fifty to a hundred youngsters like you used to come. Today those who live here are as good as dead —I know people who behave normally even after drinking a full barrel of toddy

—and some after a single glassful, begin to speak incoherently ......"

"Jeevabhai, if you leave this town, do you think the people here would change?"

"No, sir, that is not what I mean. It is just that we cannot witness the death of a person whom we know. If an unknown person dies, we do not even notice it. At present, I feel, everything is dying slowly and gradually! Sometimes I feel like giving them our strongest toddy if only to make them come alive ...... alive ......"

Aalok felt that he was not Jeeva Kalal but a philosopher. He had his own philosophy and his own interpretations of life and death. But would he be able to apply his own philosophy to himself? Perhaps that would be his biggest failure ...... Could it be that liveliness had disappeared from the whole world or had it merely deserted him? Jamna humming a tune was busy preparing tea inside the hut .... Chhanalal was lost in thoughts of his Bombay theatre days and his Vilasvati ... he had forgotten his part in the drama of life ... and while Jeeva Kalal remembered his part well, he did not have a stage to perform it on.

Jamna brought in the cups of tea. While drinking his tea, Chhanalal invited Jeeva Kalal and Jamna and insisted that they attend the night show at the theatre.

"Today's play is being staged after a long time. It is titled *Bhut Rade Bhenkar (Lonely Cries of the Ghost)*. You must be aware of the Mangdawalla story; the play is based on that story ......"

Aalok had a feeling that the fiery light being reflected on the toddy palm leaves was slowly spreading, engulfing the whole of the forest and then just as slowly the whole fire disappeared; the only thing that remained was the ghost city of Mangdawalla. The shadowless ghost of the young man, who showered his hospitality on the guests who passed by his desolate and solitary mansion after evening; and during the silence and the loneliness of the night ...

Aalok got up. "I am going, Chhanabhai, I have to meet the Doctor!"

The rays of the sun seemed diffused in the early morning fog; and so Aalok got an opportunity to shake off the dew drops gathered on the leaves in the small garden of the hotel. He stood near the white oleander flowers for a moment. Looking at the unperfumed whiteness of the flowers, he remembered something and at once returned without even touching them!

He sat on the small swing in the garden that hung from a branch of the neem tree. His life's progress was very similar to the motion of the swing. Tied to one place, it could move only to the two extremes without pausing at either end ... and the alternate solution for reaching somewhere was to become static. Did that mean death?

Though he was seated on the motionless swing, fear gripped Aalok suddenly, causing a spasm which set the swing swaying. He heard a sound and watched the back door open and Christine appear. She was returning from her morning dip in the sea. Her hair still wet had drops of water which reminded him of the dew drops that were on the white flowers. In white clothes she looked like a nun. Her only ornament was the smile on her lips.

"Do come," Aalok said, getting up from the swing.

"No, please stay seated. I will sit here," Christine said sitting on the cane chair.

"Have you had your tea?"

"No."

Christine called Shankar and asked him to serve breakfast in the garden. "This morning, two new guests have arrived," said Christine.

"Is that so?"

"Yes, they are husband and wife, but not newly married. They have come here to buy some land for their factory ......"

"People come here only if they have some work. Some come here to drink toddy, others to perform a drama, yet others to practise medicine. How many would there be like me?"

"In this town, most of the people are unemployed. How many of them have real work to do? Either their sons have settled in Bombay or Ahmedabad earning good salaries or their daughters have married and gone to cities. Then why do they live here?"

"They look after their houses," said Aalok.

"And aren't you looking after your solitude?" asked Christine.

For a second, Aalok could not understand how this thought could have occurred to Christine.

He said "Christine, one can only take care of something which one has. I have yet to create my solitude, my loneliness."

And Aalok felt like telling her more: When he had come here leaving Manjari, he had not known what loneliness was. But when he returned to city life what would happen? Wasn't he perhaps afraid that at that time he would be really lonely and was he not prolonging his stay here out of fear?

Christine got up.

"Please sit, or are you in a hurry?" asked Aalok.

Laughingly Christine sat back. "I told you I had some guests, I have to look after them too! And why should I come in your way when you are creating your solitude?"

"Christine, we are talking in riddles. I was not aware that there could be somebody in this small town who could embarrass me! ......"

"If you think about this while you are back in the city, this embarrassment here will seem of no consequence. You will hardly remember any of it."

"Do you remember that afternoon when you showed me the mirage?"

"Yes."

"To see a mirage with naked eyes is not a small perplexity!"

"What do you mean? Such mirages are always seen at noon where there is sand."

"It is true that mirages are found on the sand dunes, but the mirages over here are seen for a short time and very soon become indistinct."

"Christine, I do not know why, but certain things cannot be said aloud. There are certain people who never have a certain congenial atmosphere in which to talk about certain things . . . . . ."

"In that case, it is better not to talk about those things."

Aalok was stunned at this reply from Christine. He was at a loss for words.

"Aalok, my husband used to tell me about one of his friends. A very cruel person who used to whip the workers of his factory, treating them like animals."

"Yes," Aalok was unable to guess the focus of Christine's words. He listened anxiously.

"But that man had an innate quality, a virtue. He would not eat before feeding the doves with half a kilo of corn. This act of generosity helped him to believe how human he was. When he fed the pigeons which gathered around him, their cooing of gave him the satisfaction of being compassionate."

Christine stopped for a moment, and then stood up, saying, "I am sorry, Aalok, but when we try to discuss something delicate with a person we don't know very well, this always happens. We try to create impossible daydreams by talking about pigeons' food and find support in mirages! . . . So, here comes Shankar with the breakfast tray. Will you be offended if I do not accompany you? I do have to look after those new clients too, you know!"

For a second, Aalok thought of preventing Christine from going by holding her hand; but the next moment he realised that it could be misconstrued. Christine's talk had pierced Aalok's heart. One takes it for granted that what one thinks and wants to hear is what the other person would think and say. But Christine had said something very different from what Aalok had wanted to hear. And of course, there was a ring of truth in what she had said! After this conversation would he ever have the courage to answer any of Christine's queries? There were all the possibilities that his stay here might become like a temporary interruption of a running stream. Should that happen, then his talk with Christine was more cruel than the whipping meted out by those men.

H—3

The sun's rays touched his cheeks and he realised that the fog had melted. The dew drops had evaporated from the white flowers. The swing had become static; he grew fearful and stood up.

Tikekar took out an inland letter form[1] from the drawer. He arranged the other letters and then cautiously closed the drawer. He locked the drawer with the key that was already in the keyhole and, tried the drawer to see whether it was properly locked or not.

He then held the letter in the light and looked at it closely for sometime, as if he were trying to unravel some secret watermark! He placed the inland on the table, put on his spectacles and began to write.

Every now and then he would stop as if to think, and then write another two to three sentences and stop again.

Finally he finished the whole letter and it read over atleast thrice. Then he cautiously folded the letter, made sure that the folds were along the marked lines, and pressed the folds down with his thumb. Then he refolded it a second time, again taking the same precaution. Then a third time. He then took off his glasses, re-opened the drawer and took out the gum bottle. He held the gum bottle up to the light, shook it and taking the brush from the bottle, applied it, sealed and patted the letter and carefully wiped the extra gum with a napkin. Once again he looked thoughtfully at the letter. He then put on his glasses and addressed the letter; then he held the letter in his hand to make sure that nothing which was written which would be visible outside. Then he hollowed the letter into an 'O' and tried to see how much could be read. After this he called out to the maid servant Reva.

"Yes, Sir?" The maid appeared.

"Now listen carefully. Take this letter, hold it between your two fingers, not on your palm lest it get crumpled ......"

"Yes ......" Reva said extending her hand, but instead of giving her the letter, Tikekar said:

"Be careful, and pop this letter only into the red box. When does the next post go?"

---

[1] Indian inland forms printed by the government are so folded as to leave two openings on either side.

"Tomorrow morning ..."

"Yes, but even so ask the postmaster and ascertain the clearance time. And look here, after you put the letter into the red box, give the box a little shake and see that the letter does not fall out."

"Yes, Sir ......"

As Reva was leaving with the letter, Tikekar remembered something and he called her back "Reva ...."

"Yes?"

"Oh, just give me the letter. Let me check whether I have addressed it correctly or not," and saying so, once more he held the letter, read the address carefully, checked whether it was properly sealed and then returned it to Reva.

"Oh God, now I am satisfied," said Tikekar and his attention was now drawn to the people seated on the opposite sofa.

"Who is it?" He got up and took off his glasses and looked at them.

"Oh, is it you, doctor? And Pilooben has also come? And who is this?"

"He is our friend, Mr. Aalok," said the doctor. "We have specially brought him here to listen to the devotional lyrics of Tukaram from Sheelaben.[1]"

Aalok had been watching Tikekar closely as he went through the motions of writing his letter. How very hard the old gentleman was trying to fill the vacuum around him, he thought to himself. At first he thought it funny, but then his heart filled with compassion for the old man. Fate had deceived him in the smallest matters of life!

He mentally recorded everything about this man Dr. Meherwan had spoken about.

"Sheela ......" Tikekar called. "See who has come?"

A middle-aged woman emerged from within. She looked about forty-five years of age. Her hair was almost grey, but that only added dignity to her face. "Pilooben!" she exclaimed smilingly.

---

[1] is a suffix commonly used to address other women, it means "sisters".

"Yes, Sheeladidi[1] , I have come to listen to your religious songs, and have brought a guest along too. Today is "Ekadashi'[2] day isn't it?"

Sheela smiled. "How well you remember our religious days![3] Who is this gentleman?"

"He has come from Bombay to see our village. He is a nice person. We became friends as soon as we met." Doctor said, "Tikekar dada, Aalokbhai[4] is a businessman in Bombay .... though a businessman, he is like a man who has renounced material things. Talk to him about religion and you will not even notice when dawn breaks!"

"Doctor, you exaggerate," said Aalok. "Dada, I thought I would listen to your commentary on *Gyaneshwari*[5] and the prayer music of Tukaram from Sheelaben. The doctor has told me about the two of you."

"What more can I say about the Gyandev's book which is the supreme scripture? Whenever I am alone, I read that book and most of the time, I am alone."

Aalok had heard the word "alone" so often, he thought, did he not have the same feeling of loneliness in this village? But after listening to what the doctor had said about Tikekar, Aalok had understood the true meaning of being alone.

T HIRTEEN

Tikekar had held an important post in the Gaikwad[6] establishment. He had had a big bungalow in Baroda; a two-horse carriage at the porch; and when he moved about in the Baroda bazaar with that typical Poona turban even a stranger would be

---

[1] elder sister.
[2] eleventh day of lunar month of Hindu Calendar.
[3] days of religious festival.
[4] brother.
[5] Swami-Gyaneshwar's commentaries on the *Gita*.
[6] one of the royal families of India

impressed with his personality and would want to bow in respect. Tikekar's wife was Ahilyabai and son Ashwin ......

Tikekar had very high hopes for Ashwin: before sending him to England for higher education, he had arranged his marriage with Sheela. Sheela was a girl from a Chitapavan Brahmin family of Poona. Tikekar had liked her and her father had no objection as she was marrying into a good family. Soon after their marriage, Ashwin went to England and returned after finishing his studies. During this time, Sheela did her Master's degree and began to teach Marathi[1] in a Baroda college.

Ashwin now wanted Sheela to change and adopt western ways. Sheela was an Indian wife and did not relish the idea, but to satisfy her husband's wishes, set about doing whatever he asked of her. Sometimes, Ashwin's expectations would amount to perversions, but that too Sheela bore stoically. And, finally, Ashwin's interest in her and his motherland evaporated. He selected yet another educational course in England, and on that pretext, went abroad again and stayed there.

Sheela went away to Poona and started teaching in a college there. Years passed. Tikekar after retirement settled in a house in Urad. He did not have the courage to go to Poona and face Sheela or their relatives. He had severed relations with Ashwin. Ashwin had remarried in England and had two children now. He had once sent a photo of his family, but Tikekar had torn it to pieces. Once Tikekar saw Ahilyabai, trying to rejoin those pieces and had said to her, "Bai, you want to eat out of your daughter-in-law's hands? Then come, I will get your passport, but in my house I do not want even a trace of their identity ...."

Ahilyabai acquired the ultimate passport and departed for that unknown abode within a short time, and Tikekar was left alone. He had money, a bungalow, servants, a son, two daughters-in-law and inspite of all this, he was alone in Urad.

When Sheela learnt about Ahilyabai's death, she decided to return to Urad to look after her father-in-law. She had thought that this way his agony would be reduced and her loneliness too would become bearable — but the worlds of two lonely persons are actually even more painful.

59

---

[1] language of the people of Maharashtra, a state in Western India.

Aalok observed Tikekar and Sheela. There was an inexplicable void evident on their faces. Perhaps they were both trying to hide that void from each other.

Sheela was singing : "I saw my death before my eyes. I feel I am a stranger in this world." Sheela sang with all her heart, tears rolling down her cheeks. Tikekar listened with closed eyes, but his lips quivered uncontrollably!

Aalok felt that only those people who can see their own selves reduced and face death boldly could behave and live like strangers when the real end comes. Not only in the village of Urad but in this house two people lived together, each witnessing the other's death, unable to know from which direction death would approach, yet constantly listening for its footsteps.

While talking about the *Gyaneshwari,* Tikekar also referred to death.

"Doctor, Gyandev[1] has talked about so many things! There was a time when I could recite the whole of *Gyaneshwari* —now I can only recite a few verses which have become like my daily prayer:

'Oh Pandev, one should leave the mortal frame like a covered candle flame unknowingly extinguished.'

Can death come this way?

It was past midnight and Aalok going towards his hotel was thinking : the candle burns, the wax melts and the flame gets low and goes out without anybody's knowledge — will my soul also be able to leave my body and extinguish itself in the same way? Who knows? At present, Tikekar, Sheela, Meherwan, Piloo, Christine, Chhanalal and I are all like burning candles in the shade. Perhaps this Urad village too is one such burning candle. Who knows, how much wax now remains!

But why is he staying here? Why does he not want to return? In Manjari's warm company, he had once enjoyed airconditioned comforts; watched love-scenes on the screen; he could spend his days at the steering wheel of his car. What if he were to move away from this atmosphere of death and go back to life as he remembered it?

He remembered Christine. Life is only that which moves towards death; and that which does not move, is it not inertia?

---

[1] well-known saint of Maharashtra.

The faculty of love in Christine was gradually becoming inert, and with that her life also would be extinguished and a day would come when the vessel would remain and the candle below it die out ...

What then?

He was startled at Tommy's barking. Unconsciously, he had entered the hotel and was near Christine's verandah; the dog's barking had startled him. The verandah was in darkness. He turned back but before he could move he heard Christine's voice.

"Aalok, did you want something?"

Christine was sitting on the verandah in darkness. She lit the candle that was by her side on the table. In the candlelight, Christine's face shone.

"Oh no, I am very sorry, I came this way by mistake ..."

"Won't you have your dinner?"

"No, I had my dinner at Meherwan's place," said Aalok and started to go but then he thought of something and turned back.

"Christine, I feel, I would like to go away tomorrow ..."

The expression on Christine's face was hard to decipher in the candle light.

"Please get the bill ready in the morning ......"

"All right," said Christine, "I will keep the bill ready."

And then she said quickly all in one breath, "Do come again. When clients like you come, the hotel becomes lively. Now don't come alone and pardon us if there has been any shortcoming in our hospitality ..."

Were these words spoken in pain or sarcasm? Aalok could not tell. He stood there for a few minutes supporting himself on the pillar, but Christine did not say anything more. He turned back. He heard Christine blow out the candle. He felt like turning around for a last glimpse but instead he went away without looking back and on entering his room, closed the door.

Aalok felt he had done a great injustice to Manjari. How could Manjari behave any differently considering the atmosphere in which she had been brought up? Wasn't it an additional qualification that she had chosen a person like himself?

If he did not go back to her now, what would happen to Manjari? Whatever support she needed from him would be taken away; and she would, for days together, be heart broken and depressed; she would no longer be interested in developing any other intimate relationship and even if she did, and if that person some day were to ask her: "Manjari, what sort of relationship did you and Aalok have?" What would happen then? What would she reply? What evidence would she have to prove her answer?

It is easy for a man to leave a woman; he can settle down very easily in life after such a deed, and without any inhibition narrate everything regarding his past love life. But for a woman, this sort of experience becomes a once-in-a-life time episode.

His educated mind told him that this should not be so yet it was the case. What could be done?

What if he married Manjari and was unable to make her happy afterwards ... the standard of Manjari's happiness was vastly different from his own and he might never be able to accept her standards, and consequently become reserved and unsociable. As a result, Manjari might have to face the ridicule of her family ... he would then get anxious about her and both of them would suffer. Though sleeping together, they would be far apart in all other respects, and what would happen then? Tomorrow morning he would go away from here.

But where would he go?

He could once again attend to his business and dispassionately recollect the whole situation.

The whole night passed in a state of restlessness, his mind agitated. He woke up feeling far from fresh, his eyes gritty and heavy with sleep; he completed his morning ablutions and sat at the dining table. When Shankar brought him breakfast and an envelope on a tray, he thought it was a bill he had asked for, and took it. He went inside the room and opened the envelope: in it was a small note for Aalok, instead of the bill.

Aalok,

Does everything have to be priced in rupees? The whole night I tried to settle your accounts in rupees for the period that you have stayed here. I have failed and I am sorry, I think you will have to pardon me.

These few days that you have stayed here have been made sorrowful by me. You came here to find a new life, instead, I feel, you have been crushed into an atmosphere of death. I know, I am not totally responsible for that, but for whatever little I contributed, I have to ask your forgiveness.

I want something more from you than a mere bill. Please forget everything that I told you on that fateful night. It was not the whole truth. It might have been true momentarily but then, when you consider the whole situation, the untruthfulness of those words stands out very obviously. It would be better if you could forget that moment. You have obliged me with many favours, please do one more; I would be much indebted to you for it.

Do you have enough money to pay my bill? If you do not, please leave without trying to pay me ......

Yours,
Christine.

Aalok was stunned by the letter and for sometime could not do anything. He then called Shankar. "Where is madam?"

"Madam has gone to Daman."

"When?"

"Today, by the early morning bus."

Aalok bit his lips.

"Sir, madam has asked me to take you to the station. The train leaves at twelve noon."

Aalok was confused. He went sea-bathing. It was high tide and the sea was coming in nearer and nearer. In the opposite direction, the sun had risen, its rays reflecting on the waves and seen at a long, distance off. It looked like a timid deer gambling. He had come this way after quite a while. He thought, he could hear Gomti's screams in the sound of the waves. He stared at her dilapidated house that still stood on the shore.

He undressed and kept the clothes on the beach; and then walked into the water. To reach the deep levels where he could swim, he had to go farther in for about a furlong. The high tide alternatively clasped his legs coiling around them and released them. He was absent mindedly moving forward at a slow pace. Far, far away, the fishermen's boats were visible. At his back, behind a belt of the cypress trees, lay the village of Urad.

Perhaps, Chhanalal was awake now, after a late night's hard work — last night he would have performed the role of Mangdawalla.

Meherwan and Piloo must be drinking their morning tea together, and they might have suddenly fallen silent recalling Shyavaksha. His soul, sitting high on the topmost peak of the Alps must be laughing, and saying, "So, you still have not been able to reach me ......!"

Tikekar and Sheela must be continuing to witness their own deaths; but death does not come like that. The trembling flame of the candle in the shade of the vessel will continue to burn. Who can tell for how long? At least for quite some time.

And Christine ......

She must be in confession now, at this time, to Father Velant. What would she be saying?

This time the tidal wave rushed and coiled about his ankle but did not release him. He stopped for a while and waited. He then tried to lift his leg and with an effort did so. He saw a long, thick snake coiled tightly about his leg. Aalok, using all his strength, put his leg once again into the water; the heaviness

about his leg remained.

He was stupefied. He did not know what he should do. The pressure on his leg was increasing and he screamed out in intolerable, excruciating pain.

The pressure then lessened but by then he had fallen unconscious.

The darkness before dawn had an undercurrent which made Christine feel wary that something untoward was about to happen. The dust on the road, the sound of the waves, the shrill cries of birds, the rustle of leaves — it all seemed to add to that unease — her heartbeats too followed that rhythm when she suddenly stopped.

"What is it madam? Have you forgotten something?" asked Shankar who was following her.

"No," she said, and started walking very fast. It seemed that this little conversation between her and Shankar had broken up the whole conversation with nature.

When they reached the bus stop, they were early. Both the driver and conductor were sleeping with the coach doors closed. Christine sat on a small bench near the bus.

"Shankar," she said.

"Yes."

"That sahib is leaving today. Give him the envelope that I gave you, and see that he reaches the bus station on time. If he wants you to go upto the railway station, then go with him."

"Yes, Madam." said Shankar.

"I will return by the night bus. Meanwhile look after the other guests."

There was some movement within the bus. The driver and conductor were both awake. They washed their faces and in the meantime two other passengers also arrived. Christine went and sat in the bus. The driver honked three or four times in the dark and then started the engine.

A few stray dogs were awake in the dawn and they barked on the lonely roads along which the bus passed before entering the road that led to the toddy tree jungle. It created a feeling that the bus was passing along a deep and endless void. In the darkness, toddy trees seemed like shadows running in the opposite direction. The inside of the bus was aglow with light which spilt out on the road through the window making fast lighted squares on the road. After issuing three tickets, the conductor settled down on the seat. The other two travellers tried to finish their night's quota of sleep. The driver was concentrating on the road — on the beams of light that showed the road ahead for a distance. Christine was trying to penetrate the darkness that covered her mind!

Christine now thought of the imperceptible fact that she had seen in the dim candlelight and Aalok's words were so full of pain. She could feel the heaviness of those words even now. Aalok would have certainly stayed back had she insisted even a little but now he would not stay anymore. When she returned at night, the atmosphere of the boarding house would be as casual and as silent as ever. There would be a silence without expectations. She could ask anxiously, "Has that guest left?" Shankar would nod in reply but she would not get the answer she wanted. And how could she ask Shankar what he had said while leaving or how he had spent the morning? Did he look sad or quite happy? She knew that nobody could answer those questions.

Even if she should go and sit in Aalok's room, she would not be able to distill the few sighs that he might have heaved before leaving the room; could it have mingled with the pindrop silence that prevailed there? How would his spoken words still reverberate in the atmosphere? A sad man had entered her life for a few days and had suddenly disappeared. Now he would never be seen again!

Fourteen

It was daybreak. The darkness that had disappeared will never return again. Some other darkness might be on its way. But the one which was folded in the rays of the rising sun throbbed with totally different expectations.

In the morning light, everything looked different. The bus was full of passengers, more boarding at subsequent stops. The conductor and the driver also looked different. The Sunday morning atmosphere was visible in the bus. Most of the passengers were out on a weekly shopping spree and discussions were about rising prices, the money market and the exploitation by traders. The Parsi girl who was sitting next to Christine and who had tried to draw her into a conversation kept looking at her curiously off and on. But before she could make eye contact with Christine her sight would be reflected back as if the glance had fallen on some dark opaque curtain that surrounded Christine's mind. When the bus stopped at the Daman bus station, the sudden movements of the passengers broke through Christine's preoccupations.

In the early morning the sky was turning whitish blue and in that dull light, the light blue of Christine's saree looked utterly different. Christine got down from the bus and walked in the direction of the church. When she saw other girls hurrying towards the church, she too increased her speed. She covered her head with the saree and held its end between her lips.

Father Velant was delivering the Sunday mass.

It seemed that the ringing voice of the priest had settled into every nook and corner of the church. Christine stared at Father Velant's white vestments that were flying in the breeze. Then her eyes steadied on the sparkling eyes, his white hair and white beard. She felt she was imbibing every word he uttered.

"Glory to God ..." Father Velant preached. His voice and words were so forceful that he could implant the words of Christ in every heart. He concluded:

"In the name of the Father, and of the Son and of the Holy Ghost .... Amen." He had finished his sermon and everybody began to disperse. Christine hurriedly went after Father Velant.

"Father, I want your blessings."

"Today is Sunday and many have come for confessions. Are you aware of the new laws?"

"Yes Father, but ......"

"You can come at ten o'clock", said Father.

"All right."

The priest then made a sign of the cross.

Christine came out of the church. The priest's prayers were still ringing in her ears and she did not listen to any of the surrounding noise. A motor car brushed past her and stopped with a crash of sudden brakes. She was startled. Seated in the car were Meherwan and Piloo.

"How is it you are here?" asked Piloo.

"It being Sunday, I came here for the morning service in the church," said Christine.

"Come on, let us have some tea together," said Meherwan.

Meherwan had a small bungalow in Daman and usually on weekends they stayed there.

The sea was visible from the porch of the bungalow. A Victorian dining table was laid there. Looking at the sea from there, Christine remembered what Aalok had said on the very first day of his arrival — "This Daman seems to be a living character in your village."

Christine was observing Daman in this context for the first time. It was as dirty a town as Urad. Of course, the electricity in this town made it look different during the night.

"Is Aalok leaving today? Had I known about it earlier, I would have cancelled my trip," said Meherwan.

"Last night he suddenly decided to leave," said Christine.

"He was a nice man, wasn't he Christine? We have not met a person like him. In the morning, while travelling in the car, we were talking about him," said Piloo.

"Piloo, there was something in him that was lovable and he also got attached to our village and a few people there, but he felt he had to go!"

"Did you come here only to escape the farewell? No doubt, it would have been painful," said Meherwan.

"I had already decided to come here, even before he made up his mind to return. Though I must say, it would have been a difficult situation," she shyly confessed.

"Christine, within the short period, that we knew him we liked him very much. We liked the way he took an interest in you," said Meherwan.

"What do you mean?" The tempo of Christine's heartbeats had increased. She could not imagine what conversations Alok could have had with them!

"He used to say, 'This Christine is a wonderful lady. I would like to somehow remove the sadness on her face.' Christine, because we are so close to you I can take the liberty and venture to say that perhaps he was in love with you!" said Meherwan.

"Doctor, this word 'love' applies only upto a certain age; after that its meaning changes completely! I can also say that Aalok was a nice man. I did not get tired even if we talked to each other for hours. When I used to sit with him, slowly drinking a cocktail of vermouth and gin, I would feel a strange sort of excitement from within. But then, that only meant that we two were able to talk to each other congenially. And it hardly ever happens that you fall in love with a person with whom you are able to converse!" answered Christine! But she knew that this reply sounded unconvincing even to her.

"Christine, I am sorry, I made you sad by opening this topic," said Meherwan.

Christine's eyes were on the sea. Without knowing why she was very uncomfortable. She said looking at Meherwan, "Doctor, you have not made me sad, only thoughtful . . ."

"Christine, please join us for lunch. We will then leave for Urad together in the afternoon," said Piloo.

"All right," Christine replied.

It was nine-thirty when she reached the church. At this time of the day, it was entirely free of people and only one door was open. Slowly she entered and saw two well lit candles on the altar, casting their glow on Mother Mary's face.

Christine adjusted her head scarf and knelt, closed her eyes and tried to concentrate on Mother Mary's face but instead she lapsed into a dream where different episodes of the past came before her mind's eye. She remembered the night when she had disclosed her secret to Aalok, and the thoughtful expression on his face.

She tried to remove these thoughts from her mind and looked instead at Mother Mary and her Holy Son. She made an effort to remember the morning sermon of Father Velant and his words came to her: "How much Jesus had suffered! In comparison, how much do we suffer? In pampering ourselves, are we not forgetting this fact? ..."

Behind closed lids, she saw a pale dignified man carrying a cross. He grew bigger and bigger, on his shoulders were abrasions made by the cross he carried. His eyes were full of compassion for the people who through sinning, had made him carry the cross. He leaned against a wall in exhaustion. But he was forced to walk on by the soldiers who whipped him. Shoulders bleeding he staggered forward again. His eyes reflected endless forgiveness.

And she had often seen those eyes. They were familiar. Were not those eyes like the ones that had sparkled in the dimness of the candle light? Abruptly she stood up.

It was not Jesus. She saw the man who had appeared in her vision and this thought frightened her. Her lips trembled, "Bless me Lord, for I have sinned ..." Her face turned pale, she made a sign of the cross and entered Father Velant's room.

Father Velant was alone in his room. The trees and the greenery of the garden could be seen through the window overlooking the backyard. There was a table close to where Father stood. On the table was a wood carving of Jesus on the cross.

Never before had Christine entered this room with the tremulous palpitation that she felt today. Her face was pale and drained of colour. She adjusted her saree that had covered her head. She went upto Father and kneeling beside him, said in a low clear voice:

"I confess. Bless me Father for I have sinned.

It is three months since I last came ......"

Father Velant looked at Christine with compassion. Placing his hand on her head, he said, "Christine, calm down and be seated. The Holy Mother will protect you."

Father sat on the chair behind the big table. Christine sat opposite him. Looking at the wooden carving of Jesus, she remembered the vision she had had a while before.

"Father, I have sinned."

"One who repents truly is always pardoned," said Father.

"Father, I ......" Christine did not know how to say it, so she said, "I bared my body to a stranger ... a person whom I did not know!"

Father stared at Christine. Christine spoke of Aalok and said, "Father, one night when I was sitting with him, his innocence appealed to me. I wanted to share my sorrow with someone and lessen the pain. I was unable to do so for so many years! At that time, for a second, in a weak moment, I showed my body ......"

Father had already heard many of Christine's confessions in the past. So he said, "Child, are you talking about the mark of God that is on your heart?"

"Yes, Father," said Christine.

"And, is that all?"

"I also want to say something more, but I do not know whether it is true or not."

"Leave that decision to God's Son, child!"

"Father, perhaps I love that stranger."

"With your body?"

"No ......"

"Are you tied down by any promise?"

"No, Father, it is just that in my heart I have given him some place ... some status ......"

"Where is your husband at present?"

"I do not know."

"When was the last time you met your husband?"

"Eight years ago!"

"Eight years is too long a period. Do you still love your husband?"

"Some time back I used to feel that I still loved him. But now I do not feel so."

Father stared at Christine for some time. "How did you come to love this stranger?"

"I do not know Father, but I like the way he talks; and the emotions that he evokes in me, I do not know whether it could be called love or not ......"

"Is he a Christian?"

"No."

"Is he married?"

"No, but he is engaged to be married."

"Christine, my child, this is sin. But if you repent from your heart, God will forgive you ......"

"Father, can I marry him?" she had not meant to ask this question, knowing its fruitlessness, but it slipped out inadvertently.

"Child, you are a married woman, and a Christian woman is always faithful to her husband. Such thoughts can pollute the mind."

"Please forgive me, Father, and give me some atonement for that."

"What you have suffered is your expiation. Keep your mind pure. God has not created you to enjoy the physical pleasures of life. Keep faith in God and He will direct you."

"Father, I am unable to stop thinking about that man. When I was praying just now near the altar, instead of the face of Jesus I saw the face of that man, carrying the cross," said Christine.

Father Velant closed his eyes. "Every one carries his own cross: we will not be able to bear it even if an iota of His pain is distributed to the rest of mankind. My salutations to Him who carries our cross — Amen."

Christine repeated the same prayer in a low tone, and then she said, "Father ......"

"Child, God does not give anyone pain without any reason. This suffering of yours will yield the blessings of God. In an effort to search the road to happiness, man may turn to the road of sin; but the path of unhappiness never leads on to the road of sin."

"Father, what should I do?"

"Try to keep the doors of your heart open to imbibe the compassion of the eyes of the son of the God, who is carrying His cross on His own shoulders. You are a Christian woman. If you can suffer a little in the name of God, you will not be unhappy."

The road to happiness can be a sinful one; but the road to unhappiness is never sinful. Father Velant's command was clear. He implored her to take the path of unhappiness. Christine was very thoughtful when she came out of Father's room.

When she came out of the church, she was surprised to see Doctor and Piloo waiting outside.

"How is it you are here? I was on my way to your place," said Christine.

"We are leaving for Urad," said Meherwan.

"Why?" Christine did not understand.

"Please get in the car and I will tell you."

Christine's pulse raced as she sat in the car. Piloo also settled in the back seat and sat near her. Meherwan took hold of the steering wheel. After sometime, the car was on the road to Urad.

"Shankar has sent a message with a passenger who arrived on the eleven o'clock bus," said Piloo. "Perhaps there is nothing to worry about, God will look after everything, but then Aalok seems to have been bitten by a snake ......"

Christine sat as if turned to stone and said nothing. Before her eyes came the vision of Jesus carrying his own cross; and her eyes became wet.

"Christine," Piloo said taking her into her arms, "I am sure, nothing is going to happen to Aalok ......"

Christine still could not utter a single word. Father Velant's words came to her ears: "The road to unhappiness is never a road to sin."

Sitting in front and driving the car, Meherwan could not look back but he could guess what was happening in the hearts of the two women, sitting in the back seat. Piloo sat almost embracing Christine. Christine's eyes were dry and lustreless. She was confused and sat with her head on Piloo's shoulder.

"Christine, how can I ask you to be patient when I have lost patience?" said Meherwan. "But I feel that this must be a small accident. It was a sea reptile. May be it was not poisonous. If the infection is not serious, there is no cause for worry."

Christine tried to compose herself.

"I feel, Christine, that by the time we reach there, he should be all right. Do you remember last year when Mahant was bitten by a snake and he was up and about within twenty-four hours!" said Piloo.

Christine tried to say something but could not. Meherwan was trying to drive as fast as he could on the rough road.

"Piloo," said Christine, "Once Aalok was saying that this Daman of ours was like a living character of our village."

"Yes ..."

"Whether or not, the village is full of life. Daman has played the part of a living character at least in the lives of the three of us."

FIFTEEN ···

The afternoon sun seemed to be unveiling the mystery of the road that she had covered in the darkness of the dawn.

Christine became thoughtful. She felt that if she had made the first move, perhaps she would have been able to convert the irresistible attraction in Aalok's mind into love. But had she not told him about her mature age in which it seemed improper or impossible to fall in love? And besides, Aalok had his whole career ahead of him. The sentiments that had touched his heart in the atmosphere of the small village would not remain unchanged in his daily city life. Wasn't his love like the leaves on the tree? They would lose their freshness as soon as they were removed from their natural atmosphere. The echo of Aalok's words late in the night, while they sat on her verandah, so mingled inextricably with the noise of the city, could hardly be remembered. What other opportunity had she had to see and know Aalok beyond that moment of grace? How can one be sure of the true personality of a person by meeting him for just a few moments? Will his real face be the same as the one he masked from everyone? Or was it not a mask at all?

Despite all this, she might have been able to live with Aalok beause as a person he was quite different from others men. To him, the definition of a woman was not merely her body. Had it been so, he would not have stayed on in the company of an ugly deserted woman as if his life depended on her!

And what did she have to give him?

A few puzzling questions, a few sad stories of the past, a few black clouds ......

Should that time come when she had to spend prolonged spells with him, would she continuously be able to wear the face that he liked?

The beach of fine sand spread for miles and on it the golden rays of the sun shone brightly. A flock of blue pigeons fed on the beach. Aalok stared at them. He saw that the moving pigeons made designs on the sand with their claws reddened by the sun, but Aalok could not understand what they were trying to do.

He extended his gaze but could not see very much further as a shining silk curtain obstructed his vision. All of a sudden the curtain moved and in that moment he glimpsed a crowd of people whose noise penetrated the curtain. From behind that curtain a young girl emerged and the curtain came down. This girl was wearing a dance costume and was very breathless.

This dancer sighed deeply, "There are so many people over there — it is frightening ......"

And Aalok went forward ... and as soon as he drew the curtain a little aside, he saw innumerable staircases and a sea of human beings beginning to climb down the stairs, all of who were clapping loudly. Some were laughing; some were crying. Amidst this din, a boy was climbing down the stairs.

Aalok closed the curtain in fright. He looked back and saw that the pigeons had flown away. The golden colour of the sand was turning white, and was becoming unbearable. That dancer was nowhere to be seen. He suddenly felt that her face resembled that of Christine's ... but no, it could be that of Manjari's, or that of Nilanjana's, or probably that of Jamna's ...... he could not decide.

He felt that on the other side of the curtain, it was not he but Chhanalal; but he now lacked the courage to draw the curtain aside again and go forward; he was now the sole actor on the stage: the whole world had turned into an audience. Perhaps the whole world was made up of solo actors, others being included in the audience.

Restlessly he searched for the dancer. If only he could work with her. Then perhaps he might feel a little calmer; but that dancer was nowhere to be seen! Where had she come from? Was it from that crowd? Or was she a performer before an audience?

He remembered that boy who climbed down the steps, had, without any hesitation continued to descend with a quick and easy gait but then he grew frightened. He turned and started climbing up the stairs ... just like Shyavaksha who had climbed the highest peak of the Alps! Sliding aside the curtain, the boy came in and said, "There are so many people over there ... I am frightened." He then tried to climb down from a dangerously steep corner; Aalok stopped him and said: "You may fall from there. Let us sit on the sand. The sea water will come here any moment and we will be able to get out of here if we swim through it ......"

After some time, the waves of the sea started to wet the sand where they sat. These waves made him unnaturally tense. One wave leapt upwards forming the shape of a cobra's head. Aalok grew confused, but the wave fell down and instead of getting dispersing, got entangled around Aalok's leg ... and Aalok screamed....

Now Aalok could hear various voices.
Did the voice belong to the mob
that was behind that curtain? He was in excruciating pain
and felt near death. He shouted, "Chhanalal, see, who has
removed that curtain?"

"Sir, please relax; everything will be all right now."

This was Chhanalal's voice. This was not the voice of an
actor on stage. Aalok smiled. He could slowly recollect everything that had happened. This pain, the snake-bite before that
and the dream after that . . . . . .

Was the taste of death sharp, like an astringent? He was lying
on the cot in his room. Standing beside him were Shankar,
Chhanalal and a dozen unknown people. He looked at every
one. He was searching for Meherwan.

"Doctor . . ." he said.

"Sir, he has gone to Daman. We have sent a message to
him and he should be coming any moment."

The name Daman — he had been hearing it ever since he
came to this village. And when at this stage of his life (and
death) he heard the name of Daman again, he was amused.

"Sir, will you agree to what I say?" asked Chhanalal.

"What is it?"

"You educated people do not believe in tantric methods but
I have called a snake-charmer. He has cured many who were
bitten by snakes as he has been able to propitiate the family god
of snakes."*

Aalok looked at Chhanalal and said, "But the doctor will
come, won't he?"

"By the time he arrives it will be noon. We have to give
you some treatment before that."

Aalok kept quiet.

"Sir, we have nothing to lose, let the snake-charmer also try
his proficiency," said Chhanalal.

If somebody wants to use his skill in preventing death, how can he be stopped? Aalok thought, and that too when it was a question of his own death.

"Yes," Aalok said.

Aalok saw that the noon had assumed a coppery hue. Till today, he had never tried to find out what the colour of noon was! To him usually, noon was either unbearably or tolerably hot; but today he could see that the pale yellow colour of the morning sunshine had slowly changed to a reddish gold.

The snake charmer had very properly arranged the stage for his performance. For a split second, even Aalok was captivated by his charm. Now everything looked foggy — like the smoke that had come out of the furnace of the snake-charmer; and his words were still ringing in his ears:

"You have been gifted a life of forty-eight hours, Babu!"

Seventeen

This life of forty-eight hours he had to pass lying on the bed! The snake-charmer had pressed the burning coal on the toe where the snake had bitten him. After that for sometime, the pain had disappeared completely, but then his whole body began to feel heavy. It was as if somebody had put such a weight on the leg, it was difficult for him to even move it. When the pain became unbearable he wanted to scream but instead he turned to his side clenching his teeth. Chhanalal had also administered some home made pain killer but it did not ease his pain.

He thought he would be able to see only one more sunrise, who could tell what other sunrises might be witnessed by him or might not be . . .

With a sorrowful face, Chhanalal who sat beside him, said, "Sir, don't worry, only good things will happen."

Did the voice belong to Chhanalal? Even in his severe pain and in this serious condition, he could not restrain himself.

"Chhanalal, do you remember any of your speeches?"

For a second Chhanalal was shocked. Then he said, "Not a single line comes to my mind. But I remember something that was taught to me by our village master in school while teaching history."

"What was that?" Aalok asked curiously.

"When Shahjada Humayun was on his death bed, his father, the King Babur[1] prayed: 'Oh God, give my life to Shahjada and I will take on his sufferings," and Chhanalal's eyes filled while saying this. Aalok could see that Chhanalal was not acting. Nothing but truth can prevail in the vicinity of death — neither acting nor art ... and Aalok's eyes sparkled with emotion.

"Sir, please give me your address, I will send a telegram to your residence," Chhanalal again asked.

"Chhanalal, there is nothing wrong with me. When Meherwan comes, I will be all right," said Aalok. "Meherwan has a line of success on his palm."

At this point he remembered Shyavaksha. Meherwan could fight disease: but he would be defeated in a confrontation with death. A doctor never knows whether he is face to face with disease or death itself.

At this stage, if Manjari were informed, she would definitely rush to him with her relatives. But Aalok did not want to spend what were possibly his last few hours amidst the sobs of relatives. Here, Christine would probably become speechless. She might remember her private moments with him, like a heart-breaking incident from a touching novel but she was not one of those women who cry or show their emotions in public. Chhanalal might cry, and perhaps seeing him cry, Christine might not be able to control her tears ... but he was sure, Chhanalal would not cry as long as he was alive.

It would not be advisable to meet Manjari in his present condition, physical or mental. For the past few days he had consistently tried to break away from Manjari, and the distance between the two had become so vast that it could not be bridged. If Manjari should suddenly appear before him, he might wish to disappear into an abyss, the way Gomti, the wife of the old man had vanished.

---

[1] founder of the Moghul dynasty in India.

Chhanalal was still talking; he was trying to keep Aalok awake until the doctor arrived.

"Sir, I have lost all interest in this village. For years, I have roamed this area with my drama troupe performing twelve to fifteen dramas repeatedly — and now I am tired ......"

"Why?" asked Aalok.

"Sir, acting out a play lasts for three hours. One has to face reality in the remaining twenty-one hours. In some dramas after having played lover to an actress on stage, you have to fight with her off stage on the question of her payments. (At times her monetary needs and passion may arrive at some ugly compromise.) All these things are so frustrating."

"Are such things common in your profession?" asked Aalok.

"Not always, but these incidents are not uncommon. Usually the actresses have very good morals. One of them, Vilasvati was a very prominent actress and she married the proprietor of the theatre. At that time someone had remarked that several housewives wrecked their marriages and families influenced by the theatre; while actresses married and settled for life.

"Have you ever met Vilasvati after that, Chhanalal?"

"Yes sir, but she has become the wife of a big man. Her husband now runs two drama companies. Once when I was in search of a heroine for my drama troupe, I visited her. She was resting in an easy chair. As she was alone, I did not want to stay long and got up to leave. She called me back and asked, 'Chhanalal, don't you recognise me?' I returned and said, 'Madam, I do not know you but I used to know one Vilasvati.'

She said, 'You have not changed. You have still retained that jolly nature of yours. So how is your troupe faring?'

'God is kind,' I said and once more prepared to leave, when she said, 'Chhanalal, I too sometimes remember those old days. What do you think, would we have been happy had we married?'"

"Sir, I did not want to answer her but the words popped out, 'Madam, you have enough leisure to recapitulate past love affairs, chewing betel leaves and relaxing happily. For us it is a question of staying our hunger. For this we travel from place to place — and it is one mouth less now ......' I saw tears rush to her eyes and could not speak any further.''

Chhanalal grew thoughtful after saying all this.

Chhanalal's whole world was built around failures. Whatever life there was in him was extinguishing slowly because of the deaths around him. He had been performing the same dramas repeatedly in different villages, but now he was getting tired of acting. After a couple of years he would not be able to do the main roles. At that time somebody else would be looking after his troupe and he would satisfy himself by playing minor character roles. The more he advanced in age the further the skill of acting would recede from him.

Aalok started when he saw Christine near the door. Her face was like a garden through which a great storm had passed. Her hair was all windblown, her eyes red and swollen!

Piloo was just behind Christine. Meherwan had gone to his clinic to collect some medicines and his emergency bag. Chhanalal, Shankar and others who were standing near Aalok, moved away.

How death takes a central place in the lives of people! Aalok thought. Whatever talk he had had with Christine about life, last night, seemed different now in comparison when really faced with death! He looked at Piloo. She was more composed, though sad.

Christine approached his bed and then halted. In the presence of other people she was a little embarrassed. But then, she sat by Aalok and caressing his head said: "How do you feel now?"

Aalok smiled wanly. Christine's touch only increased his suffocation.

Christine rose as soon as Meherwan entered.

"Why Aalok, we went out of town for a short while and you could not stay out of mischief! What are you upto?" asked Meherwan as he checked his pulse. The changing expressions on his face were noted by both Aalok and Christine.

He then examined the snake bite — he pressed his calf and sole and knew that all the parts were numb and insensitive. He prepared a syringe and said, "Aalok, do not worry — you are going to get well very soon."

"Christine, we will have to be very careful for this whole night. Four injections are to be given, one every hour. I will stay here for four hours but after that, for twenty-four hours we will have to be very alert and careful. If no other reactions develop during this time, then we can say he is out of danger."

"He will survive, won't he?"

"I am hopeful — but how can I assure you?"

"Should we not inform his family?" asked Christine.

"Yes, I think so."

They both returned to Aalok's room. "Aalok, please give me your full address. I want to send a message to your family."

"Christine, didn't I tell you, I have no family at all," said Aalok.

"Well, if not them, then your friends, your business partners, and Manjari — shouldn't we inform her?"

"No, not at this stage," said Aalok firmly.

"Aalok, please try to think about me — at present I am talking to you not as Christine but as the proprietress of the Boarding House — should something happen to any of my customers ......," she halted a little and then repeated, improving upon the statement, "If my customer is ill, it is my duty to inform his family."

"You will soon find enough time to carry out your duty. Nothing is going to happen to me," said Aalok.

"What is wrong if we send a wire to your house?" asked Meherwan. "There is logic in what Christine says."

"Doctor, like the snake-charmer, do you also feel I am a guest for forty-eight hours?"

The Doctor was startled. "No, I am not unduly worried about your life, though the infection is very marked. You will be bedridden for atleast a month and if your people can bring a doctor along from Bombay ......"

"There, in Bombay, no doctor is better than you," said Aalok. "All the same, let us wait till tomorrow. If necessary, we will send a telegram."

Aalok was now able to distinguish the different colours of the day. The ochre colour of the evening was the most soothing of all.

After the fourth injection, Meherwan left with Piloo. Chhanalal also had gone off unwillingly to perform in the evening's drama and to complete the preparations before the show. In between, Sheela and Tikekar came to visit Aalok. Christine had not moved from Aalok's bedside ever since she had come in at noon. She was sitting by his pillow.

Looking at the sad and sorrowful faces around him, Aalok thought : how even in such a strange and unknown place a wealth of affection had developed! But now, I have to uproot myself from this place, and either go back to my hometown or to a place beyond this life! Although there is not much difference in both situations, felt Aalok. The thought was painful. He felt as if his skin was being peeled off.

"Christine," he said.

Christine lifted her sad face and looked mutely at Aalok.

"What did Meherwan say?" Aalok asked.

"He said he was sure that the oedema would start reducing within four hours and that you would start to feel better," said Christine.

"I consoled a friend in a similar way when he was dying of cancer."

"Aalok, please try to understand my predicament; and kindly give me Manjari's address."

"Is it the Boarding House proprietress talking to one of her guests just now?" asked Aalok.

"Please don't be so cruel, Aalok, try to understand me."

"I did tell you once Christine that I have no family. Yes, Manjari has a family but I have not been able to adjust to them. Manjari however is different," Aalok waited for a second. Then he added: "Christine, today I am able to see reality. My relationship with Manjari was only upto a certain point, and that limit was so stifling that I could neither cross that limit nor turn back. And to run away from that situation was the only alternative left for me."

"Please stop talking, Aalok, you will get tired," said Christine.

"Let me talk, Christine, who knows, I may not live to say all these things another time, I know I am still not out of danger. Perhaps the last twenty-four hours of my life have begun. I want to remove that mask of innocence that I have been wearing."

"The swellings on your body are less now than they were in the afternoon Aalok, so stop thinking negatively," said Christine.

"No, Christine, I feel that the prediction of the snake charmer is correct. At present, when death is so near, I perceive life from a different angle. I was tired of city life and so I came here. The whole city seemed to suffer from high blood pressure; everybody was a victim of uncontrollable speed. It was a speed that brought only numbness; and death follows soon after the numbness has set in. When I came here, the pace of my life suddenly slowed down so much that life has become unendurable."

"I am afraid you will write a book on philosophy," said Christine.

"Yes, I too was under that illusion but after coming here, I have not been able to write a single word. I wanted to write something on the form of the Almighty, that form which we cannot see, but encounter accidentally. To try and describe it under the banner of religion, politics, social culture and to argue over it just the way blind men have described the elephant ..."

"Please Aalok, in your present condition you should not talk so much ......" said Christine.

"I have to say so many things and I seem to be running on. But then, I ask myself, is it worth speaking of any thing? How much do I know you? How many hours have we been together in the past few days that I have been here? Our delicately woven, brief relationship may not be able to bear the the burden of this sentimental outpouring; but let me tell you Christine, it is in these few hours that I have really lived, though I have existed until now masking my real face. Whenever I have shown a lack of attachment or affection in reality, it actually was the opposite — I wanted to be with you, but masked it with a show of indifference."

Aalok felt too tired to speak any more. He could not speak coherently. Meherwan had already warned Christine about the reactions of these injections and had told her not to worry, should a condition of euphoria develop and cause the patient to talk a lot.

Taking Christine's hand in his, Aalok said, "Christine, don't get startled if at this moment I tell you that I had planned the game and you were a mere pawn in it. Looking at the age difference and social status, it was not possible for any relationship to develop between us — though I was ready for the responsibility should anything have developed; I was full of doubt and therefore kept on playing the game I had organised. With cruel indifference, I waited for the death of the two wooden puppets, Manjari and Christine — and I used to believe that they were both nothing but lifeless, wooden pieces in my game; instead you have proved to be more alive than I had perceived and the person I considered alive — myself — has proved to be a puppet instead of an individual about to die ......"

Emotions chased one another across Christine's face.

"Have you finished what you wanted to say?"

With this question, Aalok came to his senses and he replied, "Yes."

"I know there is no truth in what you have said. I had felt a sense of attachment towards you which still exists — and it could develop into affection and love given the right circumstances. But we were both very conscious of not wanting to drift towards a situation like this. And vigilant people cannot fall in love, Aalok!"

Aalok stared at Christine.

Christine said, "You are a man, Aalok, and for most men love means physical desire. I am a woman and have loved — loved my mother, my husband, my God, perhaps you too in an unconscious moment, and I have occasionally loved my unborn children ... and without knowing all these different facets I love, what sense do all your words make?"

"You are right, Christine!" Aalok murmured, as if in a trance. "Watchful — cautious people cannot love and cannot live ..."

"Christine, please sit beside [me]
night as I ached all over with un[l]
ness has increased so much tha[t]
relieved of the pain. I feel sure
mark, I will not be alive," said

"Aalok ......"

"Christine, don't panic. I c
death objectively. My last brea[th]

Christine felt Aalok's pulse
it was ...... Aalok's face was
had turned blue black. She g
somebody to call Meherwan."

"Christine, please sit here,
Aalok said. His voice rang w
back.

All of a sudden Aalok felt
still for sometime. His face rev

"Is anything wrong?" asked

There was a flicker of smile
blue sky that was visible from
to compare the emptiness tha[t]
he had tried to fill that vacu[um]
everything had slipped away!

"Christine," he said.

Christine looked at Aalok

"I once told you about re
confess the truth, but the tr
extremes. I had not realised..
he paused for sometime.

"Christine, when we talk
ality we don another. I tol[d]
Perhaps, that game was not
somebody else was."

"Aalok, we will get enoug[h]
just now why don't you rest

"There will be infinite t
there will not be any time
never be able to repay you
to me and taken care of m[e]

"You are right, Christine!" Aalok murmured, as if in a trance. "Watchful — cautious people cannot love and cannot live ..."

NINETEEN

It was nearing midnight and the doctor had just left. So far the oedema had not receded. Shankar was fomenting Aalok's legs. Aalok was also made to drink hot milk.

Now Shankar too had dozed off. Christine in the adjoining room might be awake. Aalok had talked so much during the afternoon that he now felt tired and his body felt heavier than before.

The infected snake bite had been bathed in seawater, into which he had fallen; this had intensified the wound and worsened the condition. Meherwan was inclined to take Aalok to Daman by car, so that he could be treated better in the hospital there, even given a blood transfusion; but Aalok had refused to go.

At this late hour, Aalok was still awake. He was thinking about the world which lay asleep under the quiet spell of the night. He could hear the sound of the water mill, running slowly. He remembered the mysterious atmosphere, the same noise it made on his very first night in this place. Today, he was not afraid of the noise, as its secret was known to him. Aalok felt that his life so far had been of a similar nature — a solved puzzle become uninteresting and meaningless.

Somewhere outside, even at this time of the night the cock crowed. The general belief that the cock crows only at day break did not apply to this town and even after daybreak, half the town slumbered on. Aalok remembered the *Gyaneshwari* of Tikekar. This town may head anywhere, but he was heading towards his end like the flickering candlelight hidden under the vessel. When someone suddenly flung the vessel open, Aalok would not be there any more!

Who would be present at that time? Would Chhanalal and Vilasvati continue to mourn the loneliness of their longstanding

separation? Would Ja...
one day accept her w...
Kalal who could not...
dead body being car...
What would his feeli...
carriage driver of th...
letters; will the villag...
old man who always...
would he be waiting...

How much woul...
creased? Would Man...
about my disappeara...
tisement in the paper...
once?

Half the populati...
lytic tension but the...
surgery, and had no...
diagnose which half...

Aalok was still in...

His eyes were u...
near his bed, her ha...
speak and a few bro...

"What do you w...

"What is the tim...

"It's about morn...

"Have you been...
Christine did no...

"Christine, will...
the windows?"

"You will be c...
slid back the curtai...
darkness created a...
As the dewy air e...
Aalok asked, "Do...
the touch of the m...

"Aalok, you sho...
moment. They mu...

"I hope my fate...

"Aalok, please...

touch of your cold hand on my feverish head has put me in another world. Christine, I have experienced a woman's touch at different times; but the most calming is yours. There is no excitement in your touch; there was a prayer. With that touch I felt a peace settle on me and not excitement."

Aalok stopped. He felt he had understood some secret of love. Everyone builts a circle around oneself: two such circles in the abyss occupy a certain space, and only that much space is given to love, and only for that particular time can two people feel the same height, and stay on the same plane. Such moments seldom cross the path of happiness — but on the path of unhappiness we are afraid to form different circles. Then the wish is to meet each other more and more because it comforts both people. Now, the unending pain with which the morning had dawned gave way. Aalok had an opportunity to see Christine with new eyes. This morning he was able to observe her more closely than he could the night before. He could not compare, since there was no comparison between this morning and the other afternoon when in an air-conditioned room he had sat with Manjari to write invitation cards to their wedding. This morning was different from the morning two days ago when he was bitten by the snake on the beach — and that bite had given him forty-eight hours of life. Aalok observed changes in the atmosphere and changes in Christine's frame of mind. Just now, his eyes were heavy, but there was a serenity on his face which was perhaps due to the fresh morning air or some inner strength.

"Christine, if I die, promise me you will keep my word."

Christine did not answer.

The foggy light of the morning gained entrance into the room. This misty light and the light of the table lamp by the bed together cast a yellow hue on Aalok's face. His eyes rested on Christine, and the look gave Christine an impression that he was gradually peeling away the layers of her being. She wondered what would remain when all the layers unfolded? Aalok shifted his gaze as if he had understood some of the deep anxiety that Christine had felt.

He looked around him. He was in two minds whether to say what was in his mind or stay silent. But he said, "Christine, if I die ......"

He halted for some time — Christine stared at him. Aalok proceeded: "And if my eyes remain open, then ......" Aalok looked at Christine, "Then you close them with the touch of that white mark on your chest — perhaps I may be able to pull out the pain that is in your heart and absorb it — along with my soul that is trying to leave my body."

Christine was silent during all these moments. She was determined not to break down in front of Aalok and to listen calmly to all that he said. She could see the pain in which Aalok said these words. But Aalok's last request unnerved her. Was it a confession of love? Or was it only a part of his compassion?

After this, perhaps Aalok's temperature would drop to normal — then he would definitely remember the delirious words spoken when death was near. Circumstances would change and so perhaps would his truth. The two circles that had come near in the atmosphere of unhappiness would be separated again. Manjari and her family would take command of the new situation and look after Aalok, and at that time, in the capacity of the proprietress of the Boarding House, she would stand in the doorway and ask about his welfare.

How then would Aalok consider the talk they once had had?

She continued to gaze at Aalok. Aalok was unware of the agitation that had gripped Christine's heart. He was only aware of the superficial, sad expression on her face. Christine made up her mind and said,"The last wishes, whatever they are, of a person who is dying should always be fulfilled, Aalok, but suppose you ..."

This incomplete question entered the emptiness that was there, outside the window, and covered the whole atmosphere of the room. The curvature of the question mark turned and looked as if it were crushing Aalok's body.

The echo of Christine's question was reflected by the sea, and the wind blowing from it carried every atom of that question, entering the room. Aalok tried to catch those echoes ......

"But if you live, then ......"